Bolt Risk

Bolt Risk

A Novel by

Ann Wood

Leapfrog Press
Wellfleet, Massachusetts

DEDICATED TO THE ARTIST, MARY FASSETT

Published in 2005 in the United States by
The Leapfrog Press
P.O. Box 1495
95 Commercial Street
Wellfleet, MA 02667-1495, USA
www.leapfrogpress.com

Printed in the United States

Distributed in the United States by
Consortium Book Sales and Distribution
St. Paul, Minnesota 55114
www.cbsd.com

First Edition

Library of Congress Cataloging-in-Publication Data

Wood, Ann
  Bolt risk : a novel / by Ann Wood.-- 1st ed.
    p. cm.
  ISBN-13: 978-0-9728984-6-1 (pbk. : alk. paper)
  ISBN-10: 0-9728984-6-8 (pbk. : alk. paper)
  1. Stripteasers--Fiction. 2. Drug traffic--Fiction. 3. Drug
addicts--Fiction. 4. Musicians' spouses--Fiction. 5. Mental hospital
patients--Fiction. 6. Los Angeles (Calif.)--Fiction. 7. Seattle
(Wash.)--Fiction. I. Title.
PS3623.O623B65 2005
813'.6--dc22

                                                        2005022695

                    10 9 8 7 6 5 4 3 2 1

Bolt Risk

It was all over the news.

"Guitarist Adam Bennett, formerly of the hard rock band Z, was seriously injured this morning when the red BMW in which he was a passenger careened into Pike Place Market in downtown Seattle. Both he and the vehicle's unidentified female driver were removed using the jaws of life and rushed to the hospital. No one else was injured in the accident, which happened at approximately 2:30 this morning."

The accident scene flashed across the screen. The car had been transformed into twisted metal. Rotting fish were scattered across the roof, across the hood. The head of a buffalo fish stuck out of the broken windshield: Gutted twice, what a terrible fate. The camera panned the ground, focusing on a bent California license plate, some tuna, an immobile pile of giant crabs. Then it zoomed in on a single motorcycle boot. Adam's scuffed motorcycle boot. It was still laced up tight.

"The Pike Place Fish Market was badly damaged and the entire building will remain closed until police finish their investigation. Speed and alcohol are thought to be factors in the crash." The anchor woman smiled.

When I saw that, I knew it was over. But nothing can end before it begins.

1

It was two years ago and I had just finished college.

I moved to Los Angeles to work for this actress as a personal assistant. I'd book her hotel rooms, I'd drive her to the Playboy Mansion. I'd carry her bags, I'd pack and unpack her makeup and wardrobe. I'd make her calls and answer her calls. And, because she came from Hollywood royalty, her phone rang a lot.

Violet Scott was born into this famous family. Both her mother and father were movie stars in the 50's, and she spent her childhood around all the big time celebrities—everyone from Marilyn Monroe to Jack Nicholson. She wanted to be famous too, and started starring in movies right after finishing school. Violet wasn't that good of an actress, though, so mostly ended up in horror films. Now, decades later, she'd moved on to action movies. The movies she made weren't great—and Violet was aware enough to be quietly embarrassed that she wasn't that good an actress—but kept at it anyhow. She knew that most people couldn't tell good acting from mediocre acting anyway. Violet made money, became famous enough in her own right, and picked up a bunch of boys because of the movie choices she made. I had to respect that.

But I think that fucking as many men as possible was Violet's real goal—probably because she had to compete with her mother who was a total sexpot. One of the first jobs she had me do was Rolodex all of her men. Young, old. Broke, rich. She had so many that she kept what she called a bachelorette pad—a Studio City bungalow actually that kept her husband from knowing about all her boy action. He probably had his own boyfriends anyway.

But mostly I just hung out on the set of her action movie, "Defying Death." None of the actors were alone. All of them had someone carrying their shit, fawning over them. A paid butt-wiper, that's what I was. That's what we all were. We personal assistants would follow our actors around and listen to them bitch and moan and gossip about everyone. It was a pretty good job actually.

One day Violet and I were sitting around in her trailer, waiting for her to be called to the set, when she got a call from her agent. *Playboy* magazine wanted her to spread for a spread. Violet was pretty big into feminist rant, and while she was cool with being naked in films, she wasn't sure *Playboy* was the way to go. But she was in her forties and figured if she was going to pose, it'd have to be soon. Violet wondered aloud how many extra boys she'd get out of it. Probably a lot, she figured. And going to the Playboy Mansion was always fun. She couldn't decide what to do.

So anyway Violet gave me her credit card and sent me down to a bookstore in West Hollywood that carried a ton of women's literature. She handed me a list of feminist books and told me to buy them all. There I was, standing in the women's section searching for titles, feeling like a dick, when this feminist started talking to me about some chick book club. I accidentally gagged. It was my own fault—her talking to me, I mean—I was in fact holding *Backlash: The Undeclared War Against American Women* for Christ's sake.

"Here's a flyer. You'll really love our women's group," she said, passed me one and scratched her bare leg with a corner of the remaining pile. I took the pink triangular paper and shoved it inside *Backlash*. Violet could deal with it, this feminist stuff was her deal.

And she did. The books did their job. Maybe the flyer, which she kept and used as a bookmark. It took her a little while to read through everything. Then, after being silent for a couple days, Violet announced that she most certainly wouldn't, couldn't pose for Playboy. That feminist guilt won out in the end. Damn.

A couple days later Violet left to perform in some Hollywood retrospective show which, oddly, was shot in New York City—it was the kind of show that

13

had stars like Liza Minelli and George Hamilton singing and kicking in front of television cameras—and asked me to watch her pad. It sounded like a good plan. That was until I spent the afternoon there. Her answering machine clicked on about every half hour, some horny star-struck boy leaving Violet a message, but that was all the noise there was. By nightfall I needed to silence the silence so I headed out to a death metal show. It was probably Death or Carcass, one of those bands where I was inevitably the only chick in attendance. I sat at the bar and downed a couple whiskeys. A couple of minutes later this guy Bob fell down on a stool beside mine and started telling me about his own thrash band Z. Of course he'd put me on the guest list if I'd show the following night. Their dressing room was always well-stocked with liquor, he said. Well, hell. Why not? I told him sure I'd show.

Of course I got there kind of late. I swallowed a couple prescription diet pills I happened upon in Violet's medicine cabinet and a couple hours sped away from me. It turned out all right, though. Some big hairy guy gave me his stool at the bar which was level with the stage. It was perfect. I could see, I could drink. The second band had just removed its equipment and the guitar tech was tuning down a white custom Les Paul. By the time I downed my third drink, Z hit the stage.

I fell in love with Adam the second the lights came up. He was raging on the Les Paul and had this long strawberry-blond hair he'd swing back every once in awhile to avoid guitar-string entanglement.

Bolt Risk

Every time he'd flip his hair I'd focus on those angry blue eyes. He ripped through the music, tore at his strings. I just kept drinking and when the set ended I couldn't bring myself to climb the spiral staircase to the dressing room, I wanted to fuck him so bad. It felt dangerous. I could be controlled by that, which was something I never wanted. No way.

The next day, after jerking off didn't take my mind off that angry guitarist, I called Bob. "He isn't home," the gruff voice said. "Who's this?"

"You don't know me. Bob invited me to the show last night and I just wanted to tell him it rocked."

"Yeah. This is the guitarist. Adam. Wanna meet for a drink?" Somehow I knew it was him. Somehow I wasn't surprised that he wanted to go out for a drink. It seemed naturally surreal.

A half-hour later I entered this dive bar. Nicknames, misspelled profanity, phone numbers and crude pornography covered the walls. Adam was sitting at a table with a beer. I ordered two shots of Jack Daniels, sat down across from him and slid him a glass. He downed his. He was perfect. I ordered up two more, double them this time.

"This shit's good for your brain," he said, and knocked back the second drink. "I used to have this job looking after retards at an institution and in came this one guy who had a picket blow through his brain in some tornado. Stuck in his head. All the way through. Coulda built him right into the fence. It happened in a trailer park or somethin'. The tornado ripped the place apart. He ended up fine though. His wife said he was a mean son of a bitch, beat the shit out of her all the time. After that happened, he was as nice as could be."

"I love how no one has any idea how the brain and the mind are connected," I said, and then felt like a jerk. I couldn't help it. Experimental psychology was my favorite subject at my pretentious Vermont college. I spent three years with one professor reading every original writing in psychology, creating my own experiments and writing my own theories. I loved Freud's *The Ego and the Id*, Jung's theory of the collective unconscious, existentialism. I read Titchener, Wundt, Hull, Watson, Skinner and Rogers. For my senior thesis I wrote a paper that, in my mind, successfully disproved Freud's theory of the unconscious system. I then presented my own theory of the selective mind. They were really the same thing anyway. It was fun.

Adam wasn't like the rest of Los Angeles, he picked right up on it. "How about Frances Farmer. That fucked her up real bad, that ice pick lobotomy."

"Frontal lobe damage is no good. It sounds like it could be a Nazi experiment. I'm sure those fucking Nazis fried a lot of brains. Freakish," I said, then thought of Dachau. "Have you ever been to a concentration camp?"

I couldn't shut the fuck up. I didn't want to talk about Dachau. I didn't even want to think about Dachau. It was my fault we went there to begin with. I was eleven when I forced my father to take us there while visiting Munich. Munich kind of freaked me out anyway, because it was where my father's scary white German South African girlfriend lived. I told him I'd go only if he brought us to Dachau. I wanted him to see what he was getting himself into with that chick.

And then, once inside the barbed fence, I could hardly move. I could hardly breathe. I felt like I belonged there. I was never more terrified. Of the experiments, of the gas chamber disguised as a shower room. I walked into that building. I could see it all. Mothers and children, shaved heads, marching into the brausebad, thinking they were going to have a shower. Standing under fake showerheads, shaking, waiting for water, greeted by poison instead. Mothers gripping children, screams inhaling death.

But the worst thing was the crematorium. I couldn't force myself to step inside. I felt like I had just taken a knife to the gut, standing in that doorway. The ovens were huge. The doors were open. Several bodies were shoved in at a time. Cooked to incineration. I could see myself in there, cooking. I told Adam all of this. I was numb and sick. I needed several more drinks.

"Wow," he sounded surprised. "No. I've never been there but I need to go. It's for a song I'm writing that compares the foreign policy of the U.S. to Nazi Germany's."

Shit. A real conversation in LA. How the hell often does that happen?

After a few more rounds we went back to his apartment. He hadn't signed to a major label yet and it was a typical Hollywood musician's pad replete with overflowing ashtrays, empty beer bottles and dried vomit embedded in the carpet. The kitchen sink was piled with dirty, crusty, stinking dishes. Layers of dust, dirt and ash covered everything. Not bad. I felt right at home.

Bob came in and nodded to me as if he expected I'd be there. They both picked up their guitars and jammed for awhile. I lit a joint, leaned back and closed my eyes. They switched off playing lead on some song that sounded vaguely familiar. When Bob finally left we went into Adam's room and fucked. It was like his guitar playing—wild, aggressive, raw.

When I called him two days later, he got arrogant on me.

"I knew you'd call. Girls always call after they fuck me." I could hear him smoking on the other end.

"Yeah, well, whatever."

"So are you coming over?"

I was there in an hour.

Meeting Adam may have started it, but I should have let him go long before that night Bridget staggered into The Dancing Veil. White dots bounced off the disco ball and zigzagged across her face and body. Her neon chickenpox reflected against the mirrored walls like a prism. It threw me off, Bridget never came to work unscheduled.

I finished the song on my knees, my ass in the air, cunt in some faceless face. When the music stopped I slapped my ass twice. Hard and loud, the snaps echoed through the club. The patrons snapped to attention. Bridget laughed. I picked up the crumpled, sweaty dollars scattered along the stage floor and tugged on my gold camisole and matching thong. I staggered down three steps in three inch heels without glaring at the eyes that filled the heads lining the stage.

When I reached Bridget I could tell she was jittery, fucked up. "Hey, baby," she grinned, teeth clenched. I figured it was speed. I hoped to hell she saved some. That she was here meant something was going to happen. I was going to need something more than bourbon.

"Thought you'd want to see Adam heard his band's playing some surprise deal at the Whiskey-a-Go-Go a big hush hush hush and so everyone's going so you have to go you know let's go do a line." I slapped Bridget's hand away when she tried to grab my ass. She had to know by now that there was no way I was consciously going to fuck her. Her nose sniffed involuntarily and her veiny eyes shook. Her bony corpse shuddered when she coughed. She looked happy.

Ah, shit, I thought. Adam at the Whiskey. Bridget sped behind me into the dressing room, jabbering on and on. I couldn't pay attention. My brain was screaming at itself. How could you love someone you hated. How could you fuck somebody you loved. It only caused problems. There were always problems. Adam's problem with my job, my problem with his. Adam's problem with my personality, my problem with his. Hatred, but nothing concrete.

This time, I hadn't heard from him in months. I'd half-figured he was dead. I pulled my Jane's Addiction CD out of the club's sound system and threw it on top of a scratched Beastie Boys disc. I zipped my make-up bag, wiped my cunt and ass with a baby wipe and individually sealed my costumes in storage-size Ziploc bags. Bridget laid out a line, a line of some rocky looking crystal meth. I pressed the face of her driver's license against it and then chopped at it with the edge. Little white shards glistened on the counter. Too much and you'd lose your nose, a bit more and you'd lose your mind. I preferred coke. I preferred whiskey. I preferred morphine. I snorted the shit right up my right nostril. Bridget sucked down a line and sneezed. She wasn't going down for days. Her apartment would be really clean. I was sorry I taught her about that shit.

It happened by accident. She lived in a studio right under mine in the dregs of Hollywood. A nasty fucking neighborhood. Whitley was right off Hollywood Boulevard, a side street that smelled just as much like piss and poverty as the main drag. On the corner was a check cashing place where the rich got richer by cashing checks for well below what they were worth. Down the avenue stood a Motel 6 and a trash-strewn parking lot where no car parked because some junky would end up sitting in it to fix himself up, or steal it to get more. Our three-story stucco apartment building loomed above it all, halfway up the hill. A wrought iron fire escape wove up the side, its ladder used more than the stairs because we were always locking ourselves out. Homeless people picked through the crumbs in our trash on the corner down below. We were the privileged.

When this sleazy old disc jockey invited me to dinner I agreed to go. After all, Adam was on tour and you don't say no to a free meal. I made Bridget come in a traditional Hollywood act of avoidance. It's happening when you see a rich old guy with three or four chicks sitting around him and he pretends he's fucking them all. Some of the girls escape, others desperately fuck the old guy. I never could manage the latter. Not for a car, not for an apartment, not for money. Fucking morals.

I first met this DJ at a radio station he owned. Adam had some rock star interview lined up and made me come along. He hated publicity shit but I thought it was funny. The call-in questions clearly indicative of the plight of humanity: stupidity. ("When you write a song, what's more important, the music or the lyrics?" "How do you feel about other bands copying your sound?") So while Adam was managing to behave himself on the radio, this short round bug-eyed man started talking to me. Puffs of white whiskers shot out of both ears like smoke, making him look perpetually steamed about something. But he was nice enough. Then, later, I'd see him at the Rainbow and we'd chat. When one night he asked me to dinner, I said no but he convinced me with a bunch of Jack Daniels. Oh, well. Free booze, free meal. Bring a friend along.

Al's limo brought us to the Rainbow and we were immediately seated at a prime table. A rock star table. Without Adam, who hadn't bothered to call in weeks. Adam, you fuck. He was probably fucking some chick at that moment. Some Texas chick. Wasn't he playing out in Dallas right about now? Who fucking cared?

Bridget ordered double Jack Daniel's all over the place. The room swam. It was horrible sitting at that table because I couldn't help but notice all the celebrities that walked by: Has-been movie stars and plastic actors, rocker boys with make-up and sprayed locks, chicks who had their tits sliced open like meat and stuffed with saline filled silicone pouches so they could crawl on cars in music videos and fuck rock stars, or prove their lack of talent on "Baywatch" and fuck rock stars. Hollywood's the real silicone valley, man.

The more I drank the more pissy I became and I about had enough when some stupid rocker dude wouldn't go away.

"Hey baby, nice skirt. Nice legs. Stand up for me, baby. Stand up and spin around."

"Why don't you fucking spin around, you piece of meat," I flashed an empty rocks glass at the waitress, who nodded. Another was definitely needed.

"What? Why, baby, I was just saying how nice you look. What are you so angry for? Why would such a pretty girl be so angry?"

"I'm not fucking angry. I'm just not fucking stupid. Beat off."

Bridget followed him over to the next table. Well, he did have a nice ass. He should have flashed it. Maybe I would have been nicer. Maybe I could've used him. It's bad reasoning though, because it's hard to get the bastard out of your apartment once you're done. Bringing home some meaningless fuck who won't leave before morning is a mistake; it always left me wide-eyed and paranoid with the clock ticking slowly in the background, getting louder and louder, not letting up, not letting me go down. Then in the dressing room at work the next day I always felt like complete shit and vowed that next time I acted like a slut it wouldn't be at my place. A promise as relevant as those quitting-drinking vows made in college while puking into a dirty toilet.

Some popular mostly untalented movie actor came up to the table next and said hi to Al. Then he said something to me. I don't know what, a few nauseating words about my looking like Drew Barrymore or something. I couldn't fucking take the Hollywood bullshit anymore so I slid off the bench and walked by the blazing fireplace and up the stairs.

There were two girls' rooms: one at the end of the hallway and one just to the right. I picked the one on the right, figuring most chicks would go straight, probably figuring wrong. I lit a joint and leaned against the sink staring at the dank wall tiles brightened by little girlie flowers. The full length mirror was at least as wide as it was tall and the two yellow stalls were empty. I dragged and dragged, getting more and more fucked up until only a roach was left. That's when the door finally opened and this chick's head appeared. I automatically fisted the roach. She looked at me with eyes so wide that she appeared surprised about something. I could tell she wasn't, though, that was just her look. She had long dyed black hair, purple cheeks, purple stained lips. I felt the roach burn out against the flesh of my right palm. My eyes were swaying.

"You smoking weed in here?"

"No."

"It's cool. Just don't do it in here. The smoke goes right down the vent into the kitchen."

"Yeah. OK. Whatever."

The chick disappeared. I swallowed the roach and stumbled out of the bathroom and into the bar upstairs. The bouncer didn't make me buy a drink ticket. I'm not sure why. They were five bucks each and you could get any drink you wanted with them. I never did figure out how those drink tickets were distributed. All I knew was that some people were required to buy one or two or three to get into the bar. That, and dumbass tourists saved the rainbow cards for a keepsake. What a fucking waste. The point of the cards was, I guess, to keep the non-paying, non-drinking riff raff out of the bar, and keep everyone else drinking in there. My stumbling around tipped the bouncer off. He knew I was trashed. He knew I was there for the duration. It didn't matter either way, I could always drink more.

I decided to slow down and ordered a scotch and water which I got onto an empty table before falling onto yet another red vinyl bench. Suddenly I realized I was in a cage—not a cage exactly but the table was surrounded by mesh like on the driver's window of a stock car. And my drink wasn't on a table but a Ms. Pac Man. I used to play that shit all the time. I had gotten pretty decent at it, video games being a good trick of avoidance. I stood up to get some quarters, but stopped fast when I saw him. Someone I'd never seen before. He stood fixed and the crowd seemed to disappear around him. I rocked in the still, smoky air, trying to keep feet above heels. He stood there watching me.

He was a head taller than Adam, at least six six, bone lean, and wore a brown leather vest without a shirt. His arms, hands and chest were covered in multicolored tattoos with little unmarked flesh visible. He had these green cat-shaped eyes, as if he had suddenly transformed from calico to human. His dark hair, streaked with red, hung well past his ass. I wanted to grab that mane and fuck that boy. I felt like breaking that rule and taking him home.

He walked over and stood in front of me, staring hard, staring me down. "Hi."

"Yeah."

"I like that dress. Velvet. I have a velvet coat." I thought, sure you do, man. He asked if I wanted a drink.

"I have one, but you can get me a beer."

"Be right back." He smiled. Yike. I staggered back to Ms. Pac Man, changed my mind and swerved directly into that girl who caught me in the crapper. Her tray of drinks went flying.

"You fucking bitch. You split drinks all over me," she screamed, drenched black pants, drenched black shirt, drenched black hair.

"Oh, fuck you," I said.

I headed for the crapper. I felt those cat-eyes behind me. I could hear him soothing the waitress. My heel caught the carpet, I grabbed the wall, looked back and noticed his wallet was out. Fuck him, I thought, I can take care of myself. I took an uneventful piss and returned to my drink behind the video game. Safety. But now there was a beer in front of me, a boy in front of me. My stomach lurched, my skin went cold. He was sipping on a Bud Lite. I drained my scotch and water. He doesn't drink enough, I decided. Damn those cat-eyes, I couldn't see anything beyond them.

Bridget appeared out of nowhere and pushed against me so that I'd slide over. My bare damp legs stuck to vinyl. Fuck, man, I'm with this dude, can't you see that. But Van, that's what he said his name was, didn't even see her. Even after I introduced them. Good boy. He leaned across the video game, "I'm playing with this band The Roadies and we're staying at the bass player's house on the hill. Do you want to come over after closing?"

"Al's downstairs. He's expecting to bring us home," Bridget chimed in. Fucking bitches always do that, hence my not hanging around with them so much. But Van wasn't satisfied, "Just give me your address and I'll pick you up there."

Good deal. He wouldn't be staying over. Van walked away and returned with a napkin and a pen. I scrawled down the Whitley address in running ink, ripping the napkin in the process, and said I'd be waiting out front. Bridget wanted to come along. Well, it is a big place, he said.

Suddenly the first notes of "Sweet Child O' Mine" began playing, meaning it was time to leave. Van followed me downstairs. Fat Al was stationed at his booth and I wanted to bail on him, but he jumped up and had hold of my upper arm before I could figure out how. I took off my heels and staggered between Al and Bridget into the limo which he didn't direct to Whitley but to his own house on the hill. Of course.

Inside, we sat around his mahogany dining room table drinking champagne and burping. When Al went off to the bathroom, Bridget whispered that she had some coke. I told her to set it out on the table. Fast. Before he came back.

"That's not coke. It's speed."

"It is?"

"Jesus christ, how long have you been in this town," I asked, knowing she'd been around for years. "Yeah, man, where the fuck'd you get that? You'll be awake for days."

"I don't know. Some guy just gave it to me. I thought it was coke."

We snorted it anyway.

When Al returned, he saw our red noses and flipped. He wanted to do it with us. Poor old fuck. We didn't want him to have a heart attack, but it looked like he was going to have one. His round head turned red. His face swelled. His ear tufts looked more like smoke than ever. He ordered us out of his house and into the limo. He forced us back toward East Hollywood. Away from his white furnished mansion on the hill. Back to the briar patch, man.

When the driver opened the door in front of our slum Bridget, acting all Hollywood, turned and kissed Al on the cheek. He didn't move but nodded in appreciation. Aw, shit. As I leaned toward his gray stubbled cheek, he turned his head and jammed his tongue down my throat. Fast old bugger. I made a break from him, gagging. Bridget was walking away, laughing. Bitch.

But there was Van in a little red rental car, waiting, just like he said he would.

I called shotgun and Bridget hopped into the back. He flew through Hollywood and down Sunset, turning at the Coconut Teaser and up a curvy, narrow street, slamming the car to a halt in front of a brown security fence. We walked in and Stuart, who was kicked out of the biggest rock 'n' roll band in the world for overdoing it on vitamin H, got up off the sectional to say "Hey." His layered amber hair fell in his face, his flannel bottoms and sweatshirt hung from his narrow frame.

"Great dress. I've got a couple pairs of velvet pants."

Not again, I thought, but said, "Yeah, thanks. This is Bridget."

He fell back down in front of the wide-screen TV and continued watching some Rolling Stones rockumentary. Then Joe, the lead singer, came in from the apartment that extended off the main house. He said "Hey" and sat down to watch.

"Do you like the Stones?" Van wanted to know. Well, not really. I got over it fast after Mick Jagger did that lame-ass duet with Michael Jackson. But Van was hot. I could semi-lie for that. "Hey, who doesn't?"

Stuart started nodding off on the couch and directed himself to bed. Van tried to explain away his

Bolt Risk

bassist's drooling as excessive drinking. Yeah, right. Joe grabbed a couple beers and returned to his apartment. Van pulled a cushion out of the couch and carried it to the loft above Stuart's bedroom where Bridget would sleep.

While he was setting that up I went to the bathroom and took a piss. After flushing the crapper I pulled down my dress and ripped off the duck tape that was giving me some cleavage. It left a sticky stripe across my pale tits. When I got the dress back on again and came out, Van was standing outside the door with a bottle of Evian for each of us and led me into his room.

Van lit a candle and, with his hands on both shoulders, turned me around to unzip my dress. The rose-colored velvet material flopped down to my waist. As he peeled off his leather pants his thick dick sprung from a patch of brown pubic hair. Van leaned against me, pressing his tongue into my mouth and my body against the bed. He cooed while he kissed me. Then he reached over to the nightstand and grabbed something, a condom, which he carefully rolled on. Shit, I thought, too bad I can't fucking get off with rubber rubbing the skin off my cunt. But when he slid it in my legs instinctually wrapped over his shoulders and, in the flicker of candlelight, I watched his white rubber penis slide in and out. It was good enough. I figured I could always jerk off later.

2

I remember the moment it started, when I knew I was in love with Adam. It happened at the LA County Museum. Violet had given me a couple tickets to the opening night of the Gauguin retrospective with the stipulation that I take notes. She had a date and used the show as her excuse. She'd have to tell her husband something about it, after all, and needed to bring home an exhibition catalogue. She only hoped there were no photographers taking pictures of attending celebrities—but if there were, she'd complain that she'd been slighted by the press once again.

"Make sure you get the names of the photographers and publications that are there," she actually shook her finger at me. Then she passed me a hundred.

But I wanted to go anyhow and when I told Adam we couldn't hang out until later that night because of it, he said he wanted to go along too. Of course he did; Adam spent his childhood summers studying music at Tanglewood and listening to the Boston Pops. It surprised me that I never saw him in the Berkshires, but he said he'd gone to see more than a few Shakespeare & Company productions so maybe I did. Adam also backpacked around Europe as a teenager to drink, eat, get stoned and look at art. Whenever he played out of town he'd check out art exhibitions and recently saw a pretty good John Singer Sargent show in Seattle.

So I pulled my hair into pigtails and put on a short loose skirt and combat boots. Adam rolled his hair into some of my pink plastic curlers and wore a bell hop uniform, which he sported on the cover of his forthcoming album. It was so not thrash metal that we thought it was hilarious. We were laughing about that when we hopped onto his motorcycle and rode over to West Hollywood.

I had forgotten about boring-pretentious art gallery crowds. The kind that aimed a disdained stare at us while we waited among them in line. Hey, at least we weren't wearing all-black or lumpy shoulder pads. A couple people were cool, though, some buff gay guys asked if we were part of a performance arts troop.

"We're going to perform the last fifteen minutes of the life of William Burroughs' wife," Adam said. "All I need is an apple."

I laughed aloud, thinking about how funny that would be, a performance piece where Burroughs accidentally kills his wife while trying to shoot an apple off the top of her head. I always did wonder what the hell that chick was thinking, letting a junkie shoot at her head. ("Hey, you think you're such a good goddamn aim? Such a fucking hotshot! Try shooting this apple off the top of my head.") And the conversation that led to that. ("You better watch it bitch," he laughs, cleaning his gun. "I can hit any thing, any place, any time.") That performance piece would be hilarious, the more I thought about it. The gay boys liked the idea too. We were all laughing manically, which really seemed to piss off Gauguin's fans.

Once we got inside there was this immediate sense of joy I felt, being with Adam and Gauguin. I laughed because the uptight gallery goers hated Gauguin and dismissed him when he was alive. A clone of that earlier crowd now idolized him in death. Adam was so kind of frantic, losing curlers as he ran from painting to painting, pointing out figures.

"There are the pre-pubescent chicks Gauguin probably infected with syphilis," he grinned. "There's that red dog that I love. He painted the best animals, the best figures, man."

"Can you believe his fucking stupid wife tried to make him quit painting, and when he couldn't, she deserted him," I said. "Gauguin hired this guy to write a sort of journal for him in which he supposedly said about Tahiti, 'I can end my days in peace without thinking about tomorrow and this eternal struggle against idiots.'"

Adam laughed out loud. "That's so fucking perfect, check out all the idiots here. Maybe we should move to Tahiti."

Ann Wood

And I thought, if this seriously isn't the person I'm supposed to be with, there's no one.

After that we were never apart. His band was in the studio daily but he wanted me at every session, every show, every rehearsal. I tried to lay low and read a book but there'd he be staring at me through the glass, from the stage, from across the room. If some guy was talking to me at one of these places, Adam's face would get red, his guitar playing more aggressive. There was some blind, uncontrollable physical pull we felt. I couldn't even look him in the face when we spoke; every word was thrown peripherally. It was painful to be in the same room and not be able to touch him. I couldn't get my brain to stop thinking about him when he was in my line of vision. I could hardly see.

When the band was down to six days to finish recording and everyone who wasn't in it was barred from the studio, Adam would sneak out to find me. One night I was sitting at the counter in Duke's, this trendy diner on the strip, eating a mushroom and Swiss cheese omelet when Adam ran in. He sat down next to me, across from his photo hanging among the celebrity headshots and rock memorabilia that covered the wall. The florescent lights made him look paler than ever. Or maybe he was drained from all those nights and days in the studio. His hair was everywhere and he was confused—he couldn't figure out where to stash his leather jacket. The place was packed and he didn't want it to get stolen, so I sat on it for him.

"How's your brain," he asked, took a swig of my

36

black coffee and ordered his own.

"Fucked up," I said. He grinned. His phone rang. His smile disappeared. He looked disgusted. I knew he figured all his tracks, especially his leads, were perfect first take. He blamed the rest of the band, the producer, the engineer for taking so long.

"I'll be back in five fucking minutes but I'm out of there at midnight," he screamed into the phone, over the music blasting through the diner, over the voices of the other customers. "I need to go fucking home sometime this month." He winked at me. "Listen, the deal is, I'm out of there at midnight or I'm not coming back." He grinned. "Yeah, I thought so." Adam hung up the phone, pulled his jacket out from under my ass, and kissed me. "Be home at midnight," he said as he ran out. I sat alone, downed my omelet, and watched his coffee get cold.

And then at home in his apartment, all we did was fuck. We couldn't be near each other and get anything done. He had to go into the back room of the apartment to write tunes. I had to sit in the front room to work. I spent a lot of time on the phone scheduling Violet's dates and retreats in that front room. But I spent more time in that back room, fucking. It was so good back then, when we didn't know each other well enough to hate the other's guts. And still I knew he'd be trouble. The thing that drew me to Adam was his arrogance, and I should've known to run from that.

Never in my life had I seen so much bullshit arrogance displayed in a person who was not my father. Adam truly believed he was the world's greatest musician, a rock 'n' roll Mozart. My father thought the same thing about his acting, that no one was better. I thought they were probably both right.

My father, the Shakespearian actor, walked around behind a mask that charmed the world. He worked with Shakespeare & Company in Lenox, Mass., starting when it opened in 1978 and played everyone—King Richard III, Angelo, Baptista. He trained other actors in the classics, too, some of the best up-and-coming Shakespearian actors in the world. It was an important job, he told us, so important that I was sent off to Girl Scout Camp that summer, the summer of my eighth birthday. He just couldn't handle it, four kids by himself. My father felt sorry for himself because he was saddled with us. Sorrier than he ever was for my mother, who died a slow and painful death when I was a little kid. But I wasn't the only kid who got the boot. My brothers were sent away too, to soccer camp, but they got to go together.

So my father chose Girl Scout Camp, even though I was never a fucking Girl Scout, because the company's artistic director was sending his daughter there. She was around the same age as me and a girl so I kept getting stuck with her.

Tiny had golden hair and dull eyes the color of gray clay. She had a tick which forced her left eye closed and turned the left corner of her lip into a curl that resembled a creepy half-smile. She didn't seem to notice or care. Tiny always wore ruffled dresses. She looked like a plastic doll, the kind with arms and legs that won't bend, the kind that isn't any fun to play with. She didn't say much, she mostly just barked orders at people. At first I thought hanging out with her might be OK, because she had every cool toy in existence. The problem was that they were lined up in their original boxes on shelves that made her bedroom look like a toy store. She never played with them.

At her eighth birthday party Tiny opened each toy, politely took it out of its box, showed it to the crowd and put it back away forever. The rest of us kids sat there sweating, wishing we could try out that toy. She had us in the palms of her hands.

When I was at her house, instead of playing with toys, Tiny took calls from boys. I had to help her talk to them, she didn't even know who Pete Best was. I spent hours on the phone with her boyfriends talking about Aerosmith and Led Zepplin. All of those hours I spent with Tiny, and I didn't know a thing about her. I didn't even know if she had a personality. It seemed unlikely. Then, suddenly, we were off to camp together. And, it turned out, she continued to wear her ruffled dresses there. She even hiked in them. If I had to say one thing about her, it was that Tiny was unique. I'd give her that.

We were delivered by her father's driver to a campsite in a forest in some Western Massachusetts town. Tiny and I were to share a tent with this girl Lucy. Lucy was a Girl Scout with a skin condition that caused sores all over her body. They were on her face, on her hands. Everywhere. And her skin was flaky. Trails of translucent skin flakes flew off her wherever she went. I felt bad for her; she'd never

get away with committing a good crime with skin
like that. Too much DNA dropping off her. But she
was relatively intelligent and didn't bother me. She
at least liked games and let me fuck around with
her playing cards when I got bored. We even played
Black Jack together.

That first afternoon we were sent on a hike with
gear, food, sleeping bags and tents to familiarize
ourselves with the surrounding area. Fuck. Hiking.
Just what I wanted to do. I tried to convince them
to let me stay at the main camp so that I could read,
but it turns out reading was frowned upon. Too aca-
demic. So I reluctantly joined a group who followed
six Girl Scout leaders through a stream and up a hill
to nowhere, but it wasn't until lights out that anything happened. That was when the lesbian leaders hooked up with each other and Tiny pissed on
my pillow because she had to go and couldn't pry
the zipper of our pup tent open. The acidic smell
grew stronger as the night wore on and then, when
the sun rose in the morning, the piss began baking,
causing us to choke, causing Lucy to puke. That was
when we were finally able to get the leaders away
from their girlfriends long enough to get us out of
that tent. Of course, it was my fault. I took the spot
by the door so I could make a quick escape if Tiny
started twitching in her sleep. Served me right, really. And that was only day one.

But my father had to send me somewhere. He
was busy acting and trying to find a new girlfriend.
Neither were difficult for him. He was impressive—tall, dark, romantic-looking, first generation

Middle Eastern American, well-educated, trying to be white. He had a good tale to tell, including his father landing at Ellis Island and his serving in Vietnam. He had a noble history. He struggled and won. When we were together in public I was thrilled when he paid attention to me, everyone thought he was so cool. It was impressive how well he could fake it. Especially after some of the shit he pulled. One incident—which I have to take credit for—sent me off to boarding school.

It happened partly because my father moved us again—to the Midwest this time because he had a teaching job at Chicago Shakespeare Theater for the school year—partly because of Juan, mostly because of me. Juan was this gangbanger, back when rap was a new thing. Back way before gangster rap hit the airwaves. Juan, who was maybe seventeen, would stand on this certain corner waiting for a deal, Whoudini booming from his boombox. He could fake it well enough not to fear anyone. He was smart enough to con his mind into thinking the way he needed it to.

Not that I knew him so well. We never talked that much, I was just a nervous 14-year-old who just said "Yo" and let him hit on me every once in awhile. Until that one Halloween when everything changed.

I got off the school bus six stops early when I saw Juan standing on his corner, standing at the bus stop. His Adidas suit was red and black, gang colors. He was smoking a big doobie, and he sure as fuck wasn't worried about the cops. They were too afraid to cruise the neighborhood anyhow.

"Hey girlie. Come take a drag with me," he said,

41

slow and deep. I took a hit and jumped in his Caddie. He lit a stick of incense and balanced it in the ashtray. The sweet smoke clung to my hair, was absorbed by my corduroys. I inhaled it for hours after. He lit me my own joint and passed it over. "Yo baby you goin' be out to-night? How 'bout a date to-night?"

I almost choked on the smoke. I was supposed to go trick or treating with my brothers but I could always tell my father I was going with the girl up the street. And so we agreed to meet at seven that night.

Juan showed up on the corner on the dot with two pillow cases, and passed me one.

"Know what I'm gonna be for Halloween?" he asked, and pulled out a knife. It was a good six inches. It glimmered under the streetlights. "The Candy Man." He laughed strangely at that, which kind of got my blood pumping. I was scared. It was fun.

We headed up the hill toward my upper-middle-class neighborhood. We passed parents with kids, walking and knocking. We followed a bunch of boys and girls that were about ten. They were alone.

"Let's go baby," Juan whispered and pulled out his knife. He jumped out in front of the group, startling a couple of the girls into letting out short high-pitched screams.

"Gimme your candy," Juan put his knife in front of this kid's face. "Don't make me use this." I could see only a reflection of the knife through the kid's glasses. "Dump it in here now. No noise." The shaking kids dumped their candy from plastic jack-o-lantern buckets and glow-in-the-dark bags into Juan's sack and mine. Then we ran off, smoked some more chronic and ate some chocolate. We should have stopped but we got too greedy. Those Kit Kat bars were way too good.

The third group we hit from behind. It was three guys dressed like Ace Frehley, Gene Simmons and Peter Criss. Wigs and all. I figured those costumes were a good enough reason to mug them. What I didn't figure was that Ace was my younger brother. Juan didn't care. He pulled his knife, took their candy, and told me to come on. I stood looking at my brother. He had tears in his eyes. I figured I'd give him back his candy when I got home.

It wasn't anything I ever got to do.

My father was standing in the front door when I returned. He was livid. I knew what was coming. I could see the twitch in his cheek, hear the bite in his voice. He kept his cool until he shut the door behind us. That's when he let loose. That's when he became the father who raised me.

"You whore! You bitch," he screamed at me. "Are you trying to ruin me? Is that what you're trying to do? End up in jail with some dirt-bag? You're not going to ruin me, not my reputation, not everything I've worked for! "

He began unbuckling his belt. I ran for the bathroom. He hit the door as I slammed it shut. I pushed against it and managed to slide the lock into place.

"If you don't open this door I'll fucking kill you. Do you hear me? I'll kill you! Do you hear me?"

He meant it. He'd kill me. There was no way I was opening that door. I crawled into the claw foot tub and shrunk into a fetal position. I thought I could see the outline of his body against the door as he threw himself against it time and time again.

Then, silence.

"I'm sorry," he whispered weakly. "Please open the door, honey, I'm sorry."

I wasn't buying that and stayed put. That's when the bathroom door came down and he rushed me, belt in hand. Belt whipping against my body, red welts swelling on my shoulders and thighs. I didn't move or make a sound. I couldn't inhale. I couldn't breathe. I just waited him out. The blows weakened.

Out of breath himself, exhausted, he walked away.

"The things you make me do," he sighed. He was defeated.

The next morning he was all smiles sitting at the breakfast table with my silent brothers. I thought of apologizing to the littlest one, but decided it was better to pretend that nothing had happened. That's what my father always did.

"Pack up your things," my father told me after I finished my eggs.

Boarding school turned out to be OK. Better than home because my father wasn't there. Plus I got to read a lot and take a lot of drugs. I even had a class devoted to the works of Hubert Selby Jr. It was too perfect. And drugs were way more available there than on the street. I did coke, a little smack. Pot, of course.

And then there was this one kid Bart who I met

in the Selby class. He was born without a lower body and walked around on his hands. He wouldn't even wear gloves in the winter, but palmed the New England snow and ice. He was a tough guy. He used to scare our professor by jumping onto his desktop whenever he had a question. Sometimes he'd ask some obvious question, just so he'd have a reason to leap on the desk. The professor always looked shaken and Bart would just laugh at him. Right in his face. And there was nothing the professor could do or say. Bart knew he had it made: Most people freaked out and ran in the opposite direction when they saw him. I envied him that. I'd complain to him about my looking too approachable, too normal. All these idiots would come up to me and drone on and on until I couldn't take it anymore. I'd be standing in the cafeteria line, holding a tray, while some guy behind me blabbed on about his heroic save in last week's hockey game. Or I'd be standing in the library, waiting to check out Saul Bellow, and some chick would start talking about messages hidden in some Stephen King book. After listening to this shit for awhile—all the while getting madder—I'd be forced to tell the talkers to shut the fuck up so that they'd leave. Then I'd hear them call me a bitch as they turned away. Finally. So I was jealous of Bart and we talked about how stupid people were while we smoked out. But then, I was always smoking out. I was pretty much stoned all the time there, so I figured my father had done me a favor by sending me away. And by the time a dorm mate down the hall died after doing a speedball,

I'd learned all the lessons I'd need. There was no way I'd ever OD now.

I snorted another line before leaving The Veil. The night girls began clambering in. It was time to cruise Sunset Boulevard. To Adam. The speed made me brave. We got in Bridget's car and flew toward the Whiskey. I thought, oh fuck, I love that boy. I couldn't get him out of my head. I could feel the speed starting to run around inside me when we were coming up on Sunset Strip. Bridget was still talking away when we reached the Whiskey-a-Go-Go. She parked on a tilted side street and cranked her wheel into the curb. A line of various types of heavy metal fans wound around the Whiskey. Girls with big hair, black jeans and white high heels stood with tattooed boys in wife beater T-shirts. I don't wait in lines so we went over to the Rainbow to have a drink or few and found seats at the bar's end where we could watch people coming through the door. Some Mexican dude was bartending and my first whiskey was short so I tipped him high. The next pour, thirty seconds later, was better. Bridget couldn't sit still. She did too much fucking speed, man. The two lines I did was enough; I couldn't get drunk but was instead really thirsty and jonezing for a smoke. I ordered a beer and bought a pack of Camels from the vending machine. As I drank and chain-smoked, I eyed the clock—every time I failed to pay keen attention to the time on speed it zipped by and I missed what I intended to do. That's how I lost Adam to begin with. I didn't want that to happen again. This time, my speed-brain decided, I'd go wherever he wanted, do whatever he wanted.

Just then Bridget bounced away and around the bar. When I turned on the stool to try and keep tabs on her, some waitress knocked right into me. Her tray slid over and the beer from one bottle drenched my leather skirt, the other drained down into one of my thigh-high fuck-me boots.

"Hey," I started, and looked at her. Dyed black hair, black lipstick—that fucking chick from the jane's room I spilt drinks on ages ago. "Look, you bitch. Now we're even. OK? Stay the fuck away." I pulled off my boot and poured a drizzle of beer on the floor.

"Sorry, I didn't mean it. Honest." She held out her hand. "I'm Zelda."

"Cool." I told her my name and we shook on it. I'd dry out soon enough and I was used to smelling like booze anyway.

"Hey, you work at The Veil, right? You work with Joey?" I hadn't thought about Joey in awhile.

When Joey began as a stripper she had her own body. She had this real pretty face with magnetic blue eyes, puffy lips and long white ringlets. The problem was that she had an hour glass figure, minus the tits. So she disappeared for awhile and came back with these gargantuan tits. They were so huge that bright red stretch marks ran from her nipple down the full length of each one in several places. And you could see exactly where her tits had been sliced open.

Ann Wood

Guys dug it.

Her first day back was Christmas and the joint was dead. It seemed some Hollywooders did have families, or pretended to. We sat around for an hour without a john in sight and all kind of decided to bail for awhile. We followed the smelly Lebanese manager to his house and watched him shove an entire roasted chicken down his gullet. It was the only time I'd ever been to a Middle Eastern household and not been offered food. What a cheap lazy fuck. After he finished sucking each bone and watching some lame flick on TV we returned to The Veil.

Asian tourists, waiting outside, shuffled into the club. While it was a regular day at the office for the rest of us, Joey made some unheard of amount of cash, something like a grand. A half night's work and her new tits were nearly paid off.

A couple days later, an aging rocker named Simon Starr came in and bought her for a hundred bucks. He took her down the boulevard to his recording studio so she could dance for his guitar player's birthday. Starr then asked her out to some restaurant-hotel for a lunch-fuck. I hoped for her sake that ugly bastard wore twenty condoms. His reputation required it. Still, his long-time girlfriend-wife never figured it out. A little while later at some party she bragged that he never, ever cheated on her. I almost choked on my spit, I laughed so hard.

Anyhow, I hadn't seen Joey for a while. She had been fired—which meant she'd be back in a month or so—for kicking some other chick's ass.

We worked with this really bitchy chick from Italy.

Bolt Risk

She had this fried rusty blond hair, jet black pussy and armpit fur. Pretty much everyone disliked Eva because she wouldn't shave her pits, had a Hollywood Walk of Fame star tattooed on her arm, lectured on alcoholism, and was obsessed with Vince Neil.

One night Eva and Joey were both in the dressing room, an entirely too narrow rectangle with a mirror hanging above the length a long white counter. Metal chairs were shoved together in front of the mirror and a red velvet curtain separated the strippers from the boys. It was a weekend and Joey and the unfortunate foreigner were squished together in the room when Eva mumbled something unintelligible that Joey decided was an insult. Joey sprang up, lifted her chair in the air and smashed it over the chick's head. Eva screamed as blood ran from a gash above her ear. Joey dropped the chair and, for good measure, belted her in the nose. Eva went down. Joey went home. But we all knew that, unlike the Italian, she'd be back soon enough.

But that fight, if you can call it that, wasn't unusual. Appropriate behavior, which meant keeping to yourself, was a lesson new strippers were slow to learn. I thought that odd, maybe because I didn't have to be a stripper to figure it out. That happened when I was ten. That was when my father landed a teaching gig at the Tisch School of the Arts and moved us to New York City and more new schools. I got stuck going to this place that specialized in fifth and sixth grade, which meant I'd never see any of my brothers. Not even the mean one. Everyone there was the same and I was pretty much disgusted by them all. The teachers were watery and religious. The students wore alligators on their shirts, socks and sweaters. They were into sports, television, pop music and school dances.

I could pretty much ignore them all during class. The teachers were busy obsessing about their own lives. The students were busy gossiping by note-swapping and whispering, probably about the deformed kid, the third-world scholarship girl and me. I just sat there and read books. I was bored by *The House of Seven Gables*, kind of liked *Johnny Tremain* and read Mary Shelley's *Frankenstein* twice in one day. That afternoon I got into an argument with a science teacher who wouldn't believe that Frankenstein was the doctor, not the monster.

Lunch was a real problem, though. It was an unusually long social activity, fifty minutes. Probably to give the teachers time to call their therapists. And after we ate, the cafeteria workers corralled us outside and into the courtyard, no matter the weather. Mostly I just sat against the school building, as far away as I could get from everyone else, and read *Spy in the House of Love* or maybe *The Inferno*.

Then one day my father asked me about school.

"Have you met Bruce Paltrow's daughter," he wanted to know at dinner over kibbie and rice.

"Nope," I said.

"Who have you met?"

"No one," I said.

His face went red. "How could you meet no one," he wanted to know.

Bolt Risk

I shrugged.

He shook his head and grunted, disgusted. He lived by the theory that whoever collects the most people wins.

The next morning he decided to take me to school and stopped at a bakery along the way. He handed me a fifty dollar bill and told me to go in and get a box of cookies. He waited in the cab, double parked at the curb.

When I brought the string-tied box of fancy cookies back to him and tried to hand him the change, he surprised me.

"Keep it," my father said. "And share these at lunch."

So I felt I had to walk into that cafeteria and sit with some girls and deal with it. I figured I may as well make it the higher-ends for my father's sake. So I asked a group of pretty girls with feathered hair who wore Bonnie Bell lipsmacker in various flavors if they wanted some cookies. They grabbed them from the box and when I sat down with them, got up and moved to the other side of the room, laughter and crumbs shooting from their mouths along the way.

After that I decided not to bother with anyone. But if I ever had to, I vowed to hang with the out-casts. At least they had some class.

The same plan worked perfectly in the stripper world too. I didn't bother them, they didn't bother me. Until I was there long enough that new girls appeared, long enough to become a fixture, long enough to make friends with Bridget.

None of the girls ever deemed Bridget a threat, which was one of the things I liked about her. She was an accepted outcast. It was probably because she was too thin. She didn't have an ounce of body fat. Bones replaced hips, a ribcage replaced breasts. But she was a sensual dancer and it was obvious that she loved to fuck, and do drugs. The other strippers admired that shit. Most of her dances had her gyrating on the stage floor for a dollar or two. She never minded that. And she never minded when I told her it was possible to be too thin and tried to convince her to eat up. Not that she'd do it. Bridget was just who she was, bones and all, and that's all there was to it. The amazing thing was that she and Joey, who hated everybody, got along well because they were so opposite. Neither had a reason to be jealous of the other.

So this waitress Zelda told me that Joey was in Vegas dancing for awhile and was about to return anytime.

"You live in her building, right?" I had to admit I did. "Hey, I'm subletting her apartment. We'll have to hook-up sometime."

"Sure, whenever. I'm on the third floor, just give me a holler."

Fucking flaky LA. From hated to friendship all over a few spilt drinks.

I grabbed Bridget as she tried to run upstairs again and pointed to the clock. The opening bands had to be done by now, it was time to head over. She was twisted, she didn't want to go. She had been sitting with Shane Cox, a forth-rate bassist in a trendy hair band, and didn't want to let him go. He was cute, I'd give him that, but Bridget and I had laughed at the television just last week when he was being interviewed by MTV and got the name wrong of a Beatles cover his band recently recorded. Forget brain surgeons, he was dumber than a psych nurse.

"But Shane Cox and I were talking and he wants to know about this bass guitar I have you know the one Tom left but really what he wants to do is fuck me I can tell I wonder if we should just do it in the bathroom what da you think?"

"Come on babe, give me a fucking break. It's the drugs. You don't even like that guy. He's in that lame schlock-rock band, whatever it's called. Let's go."

She trailed me out, dismal—jittery but silent.

At least I thought she was trailing me. Bridget was definitely behind me when I walked into the Whiskey, but by the time I reached the stage she was gone. I probably lost her somewhere by the bar. Or maybe it was the bathroom. Or maybe she went back to find Shane Cox. It didn't matter, I had somewhere to go. I had someone to find.

"Jesus Christ," Adam said, when he saw me looming in the doorway of the blood-red dressing room.

He was alone—leaning against a wall greedily smoking a cigarette while shoving extras behind each ear as he always does before he goes on. He took a swig of beer, held it in his throat and gurgled the scale to warm up his voice. It made me smile.

I loved how he did that. The other guys must be backstage, waiting. Adam's fucking moodiness always had them starting late, always had the fans on edge. He spit beer and phlegm onto the floor.

"Figured you were dead," I said.

"Not that lucky. Just alone for a week in fucking Hawaii. Puts things in perspective," he said, and I couldn't believe he was still mad about my missing some fucking trip. "We're up. I can't hang with you."

"Yeah, man, that's cool. So I'll see you later."

"Later." He walked out. Bastard. I figured I'd watch him jam for awhile and then meet him back at his place. That was usually how it worked.

As it turned out, I permanently lost Bridget during that dressing room detour. I ended up roaming around the Whiskey pushing people out of the way for a half-hour looking for her. Finally I gave up and sat at the bar staring at Adam while draining a couple Long Island ice teas. What a nasty drink. It must be a nasty place. Don't chicks in Long Island have even bigger hair than heavy metal chicks? Or maybe I'm thinking of New Jersey. The set was nearly over. I watched a bunch of chicks up front swooning over the band. Heads tilted up, bodies arched up, mouths agape. There's no other world in which guys get so much free pussy. Writers used to get that shit, but now writing is passé. Pretty funny. I mean, how many chicks did Hemingway fuck? Mailer? Bukowski? Lucky timing. Lucky bastards.

I scanned the crowd for Bridget one more time. I finally gave up and went out to check on the car.

54

Bolt Risk

It was gone. Fucking bitch. All there was left to do was hang out at some dive bar and drink or hike a few blocks over to Adam's place. I chose the latter. He'd be there in about thirty-seconds speed-time anyway.

I finally moved in with Adam—which seemed like forever ago now—after he signed to a major label and before he went on Z's first world tour. I was always at his place anyway. To appease my mind, I kept my apartment and vowed to return after he left. We had only a few weeks and then six months before we could be together again, the thought of which made me want him more. I wanted to touch Adam. His long, thin body. His long, red hair. His guitar string tattoos. His perfectly beautiful cock which veered to the left, always making me come in a stroke or two.

Then, one night, I was smoking a joint in the bus while it was being unloaded by the band and its roadies. Adam and I had been together for awhile and it was his last night before heading out. The band was playing Gazzari's which, unbeknownst to us, would close in less than a year. Adam came aboard every once in a while to take a hit and kiss me. This kind of bemused smile crossed his lips whenever he looked at me sitting there.

I decided to grab a drink inside the Rainbow while Adam decided which guitars he wanted to use, how each guitar needed to be tuned. I figured I'd meet him in the dressing room after a couple. I stepped inside, plopped down on a stool and ordered a scotch on the rocks. I dropped a five before I heard a voice beside me.

"Going to see Z?" Ah, shit. It was fat Al. I hadn't seen him since that night he kicked us out of his place for not sharing speed. His ears were still smoking. "Would you like to join me for dinner?"

"Thanks, I already ate," I lied, draining my drink. Then Bridget appeared beside me.

"Hey I heard Adam's playing. I heard his band's looking pretty good too." Damn strippers. I pulled a newly lit smoke from between her lips, took a drag, downed my drink and ditched her. She ran after me on Sunset, yelling words I couldn't hear.

Adam looked up from his guitar and his smoke. He grinned at me first with his eyebrows, then with his lips. He stopped playing to move another guitar which was sitting beside him onto the floor. I kissed him on the forehead and sat against him. He really looked beautiful, with relaxed eyes. He took a pull off a Rolling Rock, lit another smoke and grinned at me.

"This is a big show, baby. Been sold out for weeks."

"Yeah, man, it's packed out there." He smiled and leaned over to kiss me. Then stood and started to walk off. He stopped in the doorway "Hey."

I caught the velvet box he tossed me. In it was a gold ring. I looked up, but he was already gone. I put it on a left finger, threw the box aside and ran out to see the show.

He started playing the riff of a single everyone knew, and the room became a collective scream.

Bolt Risk

He stepped up to the mic, "How about it." More screaming. He stepped back from the mic. His chin bobbed slowly, his eyes coolly scanned the room.

The band kicked in, sound exploded. The audience yelled the lyrics. The room vibrated. Adam flung his head back, his hair went flying. He raged with seriousness. Finally, he nodded to the new bassist, ending the song. Adam stared at the fans, staring them down. Then half-grinned.

After many more drinks and a couple more songs I realized I couldn't hear anymore, couldn't see anymore. I had to get out of there fast. I leaned on people to stay vertical and pushed through them to get outside.

The cool air hit me and I fell onto the street—my knee hit the payment, my palms hit the pavement, my head hit the pavement. No one was outside. I could hear the band in the distance. Then my name.

I followed her voice, leading me into a loud bar. I swerved after her into the kitchen, into the bathroom. Everything looked dim, I felt dim. My head shook.

Then I realized Bridget was whispering something. No, she was moaning. Fists whacked against the other side of the bathroom door. My bare ass was frozen against the metal specimen shelf above the toilet, my legs were spread as wide as the narrow space would allow. My skirt was crumpled at my waist. Her teeth were sinking into me, her tongue snaking around and in and out. Someone hollered and kept pounding on the door. Pounding and pounding. It pounded me into consciousness and I wondered why Bridget was fucking me. I shoved her head back, pushed her aside, pulled down my skirt and opened the door.

Adam was standing outside of the bathroom, red-faced. He came after me, screaming, swearing, "You fucking cunt. What the fuck was that? What the fuck was that?" The Mexican cooks laughed aloud. I stomped straight past him and into the bar. Adam followed close behind. The barkeep dropped us each a glass of Jameson's.

I sat on a square red stool and stared at the rock-schlock memorabilia hanging across from me. I heard some guy talking to Adam, something about the show tonight. Adam told him to get the fuck away. I loved that about him, his misanthropic attitude, I felt it well up inside me. I was glad I couldn't see my face through the Miller Genuine Draft slogan painted across the mirror. I could feel Adam next to me. That was enough. I didn't want to see my face, his face, our ugly faces. I leaned away from him and feigned interest in the fish in the tank. Those bluish-purple fish hovered in the water, immortal. Immoral.

"What the fuck was that," I heard Adam growl with hot whiskey-breath. I lifted the glass, drained it and threw it at the wall. It smashed against the mirror. Seven years bad luck. I wasn't expecting anything else anyway. Adam stood up and walked out. I bailed after he left, before the manager could figure out who caused what.

We followed each other to his drummer's house. Stoner was some kind of certified minister, maybe a rock 'n' roll minister or Satanic minister, which I couldn't tell. Stoner said tonight was not the right night.

"Dude, the moon is in Gemini. This is the worst fucking time to get married," he said.

"Shut the fuck up with your satanic shit and do it," Adam said. I yelled at Adam about getting married, he yelled back. I cried, he dried my face. Stoner rang a bell.

"In the name of Satan, ruler of the earth, true god, almighty and ineffable, who hast created man to reflect in thine own image and likeness, we invite the forces of hell and thrash metal to bestow their infernal power on us. Come forth to greet us and confer dark blessings upon this couple who desire to become as one in the eyes of Lucifer," Stoner sang, eyes half-closed. He drank from a chalice and called out the names of the four crowned princes from hell. I thought of Black Sabbath, how it was Adam's favorite band, how that could have something to do with this. Stoner drew a circle around us, and we said our "I dos" to become one in the eyes of Satan. Finally Stoner shouted "Hail Satan!" and handed us some forms to sign. They were already filled out. Adam was prepared.

We went home and made love. That was the first time I ever accepted that idea, making love. I had always thought it was some stupid phrase middle America used so that its collective Christian conscious could fuck. But this time I felt like Adam and I belonged together. Maybe we'd been together enough to move in perfect harmony without thought. Maybe it was true love. Probably it was just the drugs. Adam whispered that he never wanted to be with anyone else, I held my breath. We were married in every sense. It was disturbing.

3

As his departure grew near, we fought all the time. When I wanted to go out, he wanted to know what was wrong with staying home. When I wanted to stay home, he was pissed I wouldn't go out. When I wanted to fuck, he was too tired. When he wanted to fuck, I was asleep. I did a lot of fucking in my sleep. But when it was time for him to leave, he made me swear I would move permanently into his place when he got home. I made him promise to call me every week.

The morning he left I was still asleep, and woke to a ringing phone. It was Adam on the other end in a hoarse whisper saying that he wished I had gone along. He asked me to stay in his apartment. When we hung up I cried into his pillow and drifted back into unconsciousness, my cheek sticking to the wet pillow case that smelled like Adam.

I'm back at Girl Scout Camp. We are having a camp-wide picnic under a Pine tree. I'm watching a couple girls throwing a softball, and one pitch goes directly into the tree. Out comes a swarm of angry wasps. The camp counselor yells at everyone to freeze, that no one would get stung if they don't run. I run anyway, and never looked back. Fuck them.

That woke me up. I was relieved to find myself at Adam's rather than camp. I hadn't thought about the wasp incident since it happened, and it was true I didn't get stung. Tiny did. All over. She had something like eight stings and ended up in the hospital. That's what you get for listening to authority.

Because just about everyone else was rushed to the hospital, I was left virtually alone at the campsite. And only a few kids came back for the month of August. Tiny was sent to the Berkshires to recover. Lucy remained in the hospital, probably because the stings made her skin condition worse. I was lonely. It was one of the only times I ever missed my father. It made me think of good times, and we did have some. Before camp he rented a limo and took me shopping in New York City. He bought me whatever I wanted, even if it wasn't suitable for camp. He could be OK. But that craving I had for my father in camp was much like the craving I felt for Adam. I couldn't believe I already missed him. I couldn't deal with smelling him in the sheets anymore so I packed up my shit, put on a pair of his jeans and was back at my dive before sundown.

I stayed home that night and the next day and was so depressed I could hardly think, I could hardly move. It was that same feeling I had when Adam and I first met. He was gone two weeks after we got together, and it quickly started to seemed like he was this memory of something that never existed. That was when I realized that distance is everything. That was when I started dancing. That was when I started dating.

I was horny, he wasn't around. I'd leave a message, he wouldn't call back. Then every couple weeks he'd call me, half-hearted attempts to assure himself of a fuck when he returned to LA, or so I figured after hearing stories of his conquests.

My friend Shannon, who lived in Portland, said she saw Adam with some chick at the Ash Street Saloon. Adam said she was just a friend. My pal Eric ran into Adam and yet another chick pawing one another at the Cha Cha in Seattle. No wonder he never sent me the plane ticket he promised. He didn't have any cash, he claimed about the missing ticket, and she was just another friend. Well, so was Diego. And I fell into him. We fucked from the moment we met until he returned to Brooklyn a few days later. No big deal.

When Diego left, I came to realize that I knew few people. Marie, the only chick in town I went to college with, returned to Vermont to finish up her degree. Not that we hung out so much, but we did go to Johnny Rocket's once a week to share a peanut butter and jelly sandwich and fries while we talked about various professors and what students they had fucked. Violet Scott was back in Manhattan. That had been my social circle. That had been my job.

That summer in LA was hot, dry and hopeless.

I was down to my last twenty bucks when I walked down to Sunset and into The Veil, a dive spot that promised live nude revue. It was high noon, the place had just opened and there were only two customers sitting by the stage, drinking fake beer. I told the manager I wanted to work, stripped down into my g-string and see-through top, put Z on the CD player and danced to Adam. As I grinded to his guitar, I thought about how much he'd hate my skimpy outfit, the flippant way I tossed off my g-string then bent over backwards so the guy with the five could look up my cunt. I thought of how pissed he'd be if he saw me laying on the floor, my legs spread open, right arm caressing my right leg as I lifted it behind my head: A perfect pussy shot. Maybe he'd hate it, but the manager didn't. I was hired on the spot. And in three minutes with two customers, I had tripled the money in my pocket. It allowed me to hit the bars.

I met Mark at the Rainbow that night. He was a big-time poseur. He wore eyeliner, leather pants and a leather jacket with his name running down the sleeve. He was hanging out with a couple guys in his pussy band named Parris and Riff. He was corny, but I was horny, and it just got worse when I saw him. Mark stood out because he had what always appeals to me: He was dirty with long blond hair, blood-shot blue eyes, a rail-thin frame. He was pretty and fuckable and I figured he'd have a big dick. What I failed to figure was that it might be limp.

And when I called out the name on the jacket, he came like a dog heeding its owner. He couldn't help it. He was practically panting. I kept thinking his name should be Rex—come Rex! Cum! I had to concentrate on the letters sewn on the jacket to keep from shouting out the dog-name. I managed to spit out the correct name and my own, which I scribbled on a napkin along with my phone number.

Mark picked me up at the curb in front of my apartment building at ten. I swung my heels into the car and slammed the door, forcing a shiver out of the tiny white hatchback. "We have some errands to run," he said, swerving down Whitley, looking at my legs instead of the road. Yeah, OK, so my skirt was a little short. He lit a joint and passed it to me. Los Angeles is bad enough without having to drive through it sober, I figured, so I pretty much smoked the whole thing down by the time we pulled up to a Sunset motel. I followed Matt inside, staggering upstairs in dangerous shoes.

The second-floor door was answered by a stringy-haired blond chick and matching dude both of whom ran circles around the room. The double beds were covered with clothing, paperwork, an open briefcase, a bunch of empties, a fax machine. On the desk there was a boxy motel phone with a curly cord extending out of it, a rolled-up twenty dollar bill, a bunch of change. The chick couldn't stop talking. "Here Mark I rolled a joint for you I know you love the stuff whenever I get a bag I save some for you where the fuck did I put that lighter oh here it is and this is for you where's the fucking stuff?"

She slid the little jewelry bag filled with white grit down into her jeans, into her underwear. That way she wouldn't lose it, she said. I stopped listening when Matt laid down a couple lines and handed me the currency-straw. I inhaled the gritty powder without really looking at it. It tasted like shit as it dripped down the back of my throat. Crystalmethane. I was starting to think no one in LA did coke.

The chick did a line, climbed up onto the bed, began jumping as if on a trampoline, and rattled on, "So when are you playing out next you know we love your band have you seen Brett around at all because I heard they're back in town and I sure would like to see him again I wonder when he'll be at the Roxy next I love that club," she was still talking, and jumping, when we closed the door behind us.

I started to feel the speed running through me in the car. I was wide awake, jittery. I tried to keep my mouth closed so I wouldn't sound speedish. With my jaw clenched, I began chewing cheek-flesh.

Our second delivery was made to an attorney's condo near Beverly Hills. Mark said it was so-and-so the entertainment lawyer. After we pulled into her driveway, he reached in the back seat and grabbed his band's press kit and demo. He wanted a record deal. We didn't need to knock on the door, she was waiting in the window. He and this lawyer exchanged speed and press-kits, money and promises. Luckily, she didn't want anyone to stay and play. I leapt back into the car.

"How many more places, man. I didn't know you were taking me on a drug date."

Bolt Risk

"One more then we'll go out OK?" He handed me a joint, to chill me out or keep me busy, I suppose. Either way, not a bad call.

We pulled up beside the driveway of this schlock-rocker's house in Hollywood Hills. Adam vaguely knew this guy and hated his fucking guts. I thought of how Adam would despise my being there, how much Adam would love to kick his ass, and Mark's while he was at it. But he wasn't here to say it, to do it. And I wasn't going to do it for him. My only goal was getting laid and it was taking far too long as it was.

Inside, speed zombies wondered through the house, black eyes, greasy hair, taut skin stretched over bulging veins and bones. Some were watching the outside surveillance cameras on multiple monitors, others were inhaling speed. We found Charlie and his pink cotton candy-colored hair in his home studio fucking around with the drum machine. He'd been at it for hours. He looked me and said, "Hey baby how do I know you?"

I turned around and walked out the door, stumbled into the car, and lit a joint.

I had known this character briefly just before I became a stripper. Actually, he wasn't much of a character—eyeliner off and hair unsprayed, Charlie was just another boney, pink-headed drugged out rocker. His band couldn't write a decent song but MTV made it rich anyhow.

I met him at this office building at Hollywood and Vine which had advertised for some unspecified telephone help. At first I thought it was some telemarketing scheme. Gray tables and chairs were scattered throughout a large room. The furniture matched the walls in a way that would allow drab suits to blend into the background.

But these employees glowed against the wall. A dozen twenty-somethings with purple hair, no hair, tattooed heads and pierced heads filled the space. All were either fat or emaciated. All were wearing headphones with attached microphones. Some were chatting into the headpiece inaudibly, stretched out in chairs, relaxed—others were chatting among themselves.

It was a phone sex factory. As it turned out, all the phone sex operators pretended to be in different parts of the country. They were supposedly anonymous callers that hooked up with pathetic guys who paid $6.95 a minute on a 1-900-line. The job entailed getting a conversation started and keeping it going. Whoever kept listeners on the phone longest got a bonus at the end of the week.

"Oh, baby. I want to suck you off, suck your hairy balls dry," one tough guy in leather crooned into his headset.

"I've got a tight cunt," a bald punk rock chick said. "What do you want to do to it?"

A statuesque black man, a decade older than the rest of us, stood up from his seat. I vaguely recognized him from a sitcom that was on for a couple seasons a few years back, but which one I couldn't remember. He knew why I was there. "Can you take this for a second while I go grab your application? No one will call in. It's kind of early and there hasn't been a call for awhile." I wandered over, put on the headset, sat down. "Oh, there's just one thing. That's the gay line. I've been on it while Charlie's on break. If someone calls in, just pretend you're a guy."

He walked away. A voice cut in.

"Hello. Is anyone out there?"

I cleared my throat and tried to speak a little more deeply, "Hey."

"Hey," he sounded pleased. "This is Mike. Who's this?"

"John," I grinned stupidly. "I've never done this before. I'm just kind of, um, nervous."

I heard his breath quicken. "Yeah, John, that's cool. What do you want to talk about?"

"I'm not sure. I was kind of worried calling."

"It's OK. How big is your cock."

"Nine inches." Wasn't that the standard wish?

"Really, me too. Do you have it out?"

"Um, no, you know, I don't know."

A shadow was suddenly blocking the florescent light. It was a fucked-up, boney, pink-haired speed-head.

I whispered, "Hey, is this your line?"

"Huh."

I whipped the thing off my head and threw it at him. I wasn't getting paid for this shit.

The boney guy put the headset on and started chattering, "Who's John? I don't know. This is Charlie. John? Was there a John on the line? This guy really wants to talk to John."

I followed the guy with the papers into an office. It

71

was really a very nice business office. There weren't any porno posters hanging on the walls. I was disappointed.

"We pay six dollars an hour. Sick pay, vacation pay, insurance if you want it."

"Six bucks? Fuck that." I stood up and walked out.

That was the last time I saw Charlie in person. Until the drug date. Until after he made millions of dollars and managed, already, to shoot it all away.

Mark was right behind me. He hopped in, revved the engine and decided we should head down North Cherokee to Boardners, where we swallowed can after can of beer. I can't normally stomach much of the stuff, and I was way too high to get drunk, but thirst had taken over. After we downed a six pack, people drained out of the bar as it closed and we drove to his pad. He lived with his three bandmates in a two-bedroom apartment. Two per bedroom, two single mattresses side-by-side on the floor of each small room.

In the living room the band and still more speed junkies were watching a Jerry Lewis movie. I thought only the French thought that shit was funny. A bunch of big-haired chicks sat in a circle, ignoring the flick, talking fast-paced, nonstop. Cigarettes weren't extinguished but simply burned out after a replacement was lit off the last. The fog in the air reminded me of the freeway. There were drinks all around. Gin, vodka, bourbon. More beer. I lit a smoke, cracked open a warm can and sat against the wall by myself.

Bolt Risk

Then came a pounding at the door. Mark got up from the Jerry Lewis movie and peeked through the peep hole. He started to laugh.

"Parris, it's for you."

"What?" a voice groaned. Parris sat on a couch behind a curtain of long black hair. I couldn't even see his eyes. He reminded me of one of the Ramones. Maybe Dee Dee. "What? What the fuck? Can't you see I'm busy over here?"

"I said it's for you," Mark laughed.

Parris got up from the group, where he had been talking to some soap opera actress with big tits. The pounding continued. Some chick on the other side started screaming. It felt like it was in my head, assaulting my brain. Mark was still laughing. Parris put the chain on the door and opened it as far as it would allow. The chick was still screaming, begging.

"Parris, let me in. Parris, how come you didn't come over, let me in." She stuck her hand in and tried to shove the chain up. Parris slammed the door on her hand. She shrieked, started crying. Matt was laughing. The rest of the room joined in, laughing. Parris opened the door and the girl snatched her hand out, just in time for him to slam it again. The muffled cries, screams and banging continued.

"Laura, go the fuck away. You don't belong here."

Parris returned to the circle. The group returned to its conversation. Mark walked into the bathroom and laid out some more lines, called me in and I did another two. This stuff was better than what he

73

sold—it was like snorting shards of glass. My hands started shaking. My face was shaking.

When I returned to the living room, the girl was still trying to force her way in, but the fists had opened, causing the pounding to become slapping and even that seemed to be getting weaker and weaker. The room chattered away and everyone was so self-absorbed that no one seemed to notice the smudge of blood drying on the door jam. It looked like a bruise.

Mark finally called me into his room and onto his narrow mattress. We undressed and felt each other up: licked faces, lips, mouths, bodies. His flesh stretched over bones, he had no muscle, no ass, no fat. His cock would've been decent hard, but he couldn't get it up. I stroked it, it remained limp. I put the sagging flesh in my mouth and sucked it, licked it, bit it. Limp. He was fucking useless. Speed was fucking useless, unless you wanted a clean place. (Two days later I was running around scrubbing my apartment, wishing I could just fall the fuck asleep. My stomach was tight, my eyes felt like they were about to explode, I smoked cigarette after cigarette. I tried to eat, my body wanted none of it. I tried to stop talking, my mouth rattled on.)

I gave up trying to fuck Mark and returned to the living room, looked at the clock. I realized it was afternoon already. I walked out onto the balcony and saw traffic stalled on Hollywood. I was only five blocks from home.

I heard the water spray from the bathroom's showerhead and picked up my heels to make my escape. I walked by the zombies, unnoticed. What I didn't figure was that that girl would still be outside the door.

She was about fifteen, chubby and wearing a tight red rubber outfit which forced her small tits to pop out the top. Black makeup dripped down her bloated cheeks, black tears streaking her baby face. Dried blood covered her right knuckle. She really was just a kid.

She tripped up into a vertical position when I opened the door.

"Wait, wait, don't shut the door, let me in."

"You don't want to be in there." The lock clicked in place behind me.

"Do you have a phone, I just need to use a phone." She was choking back more tears. Jesus.

"Yeah. Come on."

The sun blinded me as ageless Angelyne flaunted fake tits from giant billboards, showing off for all the Asian tourists, broke rocker dudes and the dread-locked homeless guys. Angelyne. Whoever the fuck that was. Someone told me that Angelyne was just a chick who got a butt load of cosmetic surgery. Her giant tits then allowed her to marry some billionaire who spent his money promoting her on billboards throughout Hollywood. Angelyne didn't try to do anything but pose on posters, as far as I could tell.

We walked by tourist shops selling Hollywood in the form of postcards, T-shirts and aluminum Os-cars for best father. That Oscar was just fucking perfect, I thought. Maybe I'd mail one home to my father. It was the perfect insult. I decided it really wasn't worth it, though, because he wouldn't get it. He'd just see me as a fucking slow-brain who was tacky enough to buy a Shakespearean actor a fake Oscar.

Shoppers sat in the window of Hamburger Hamlet, downing fries and burgers, staring at groups of Hollywood's finest eating out of the garbage as the rock shop beside it blasted some nauseating Extreme tune. The El Capitan Theatre stood as the only building on the boulevard reminiscent of old Hollywood, with spotlights lining the sidewalk in front of its glittering sign. Down a half-block a homeless, strung-out teenager begged for money in a paper cup.

Laura moved to LA six months before because her sister was here, a sister who had since disappeared. She lived at some Jewish lawyer's house in Beverly Hills, where she was supposedly working as a maid.

"He's always looking for pale blond girls. He told me to look out for one. He might like you. You're not super-blond but you don't look like a Jew and that's what he mostly cares about. He's got a lot of money. He gave me three hundred bucks yesterday after I sucked him off."

"Hey, man. Give me a break. I'm not into that shit. Why are you trying to hang around Parris? He's treating you like a dick. Christ, look at your fucking hand." The cut had opened up again. She wiped a red streak against her bare thigh and sighed.

We crossed the street at Fredrick's of Hollywood and walked up Whitley. The smell of piss and pizza permeated the air. At the corner of my street was a dirty little market where you could get a slice of pizza for a buck, which was often my dinner.

"Look, do whatever you want with Parris. You can make one call and then I gotta kick you out."

"Sure."

After Parris' cast-off chick called her blow job lawyer for a ride and bailed, I played the answering machine. It was Adam. He was relaying his calling card number and itinerary. I looked at the clock. He was driving from Boston, Mass. to Hartford, Conn. I wondered whether he brought any East Coast chicks along for the ride. As long as I didn't know them, didn't hear about them.

I called Adam from the pay phone at work the next day, neglecting to tell him where I was. At best, he would say the job was too obvious. At worst, he'd freak out and, upon his return, run into the strip club brandishing a gun. He was sort of obsessed with guns. The first time I slept at his house, I rolled over onto a loaded sawed-off shotgun that was tucked under the bed covers.

Not that it bothered me, that shotgun. Except that it was cold against my bare skin. But I had felt that before anyway. My father was always playing with guns, although he kept them in a safe rather than in a bed. Maybe he was afraid someone would turn his own gun on him. Maybe he was afraid it'd be me.

My father liked to use guns to make threats. When he heard I had an Israeli boyfriend at boarding school he decided to teach me how the homeland-less Palestinians felt and pressed the tip of a pistol against my forehead and cocked the trigger. He didn't shoot me, of course, and it turns out it's hard to be scared of much after having a gun to your head.

Adam was right about the obviousness of a chick in Hollywood working at a strip joint; that was what bothered me. But the cash kept me in alcohol, dollar pizza and my apartment. And it was the easiest line of work: four songs an hour, cash on the spot. Then there were the stupid drooling men, the stupid drugged out strippers. But the stupidest thing was you had to tip out the bar. It was just like all those third-rate bands in LA that had to pay to play. We had to pay to stay. Those fucking barkeeps at The Veil forced us to give them twenty percent of our general tips and more for table dances. But you did what you had to do. And as long as you didn't prostitute yourself you couldn't lose your soul. Especially if you didn't have one to begin with.

The most obvious chicks at The Veil had regular customers who gave them credit cards and jewelry. Those regulars were really pathetic guys, the type who could never find a chick to fuck or marry, and didn't have anybody to spend their money on. The strippers they inevitably picked out were equally pathetic, mostly day-shifters who had some sort of imperfection that prevented them from working any night shifts—a wandering eye, a gut, a hair lip or maybe a hairy lip. Those chicks wouldn't sit around in the dressing room and read like I did when I was offstage, but would go out front, fawn over their patrons, and get a few lap dances out of them. Maybe they fucked those guys after work. One could never tell.

Bridget, on the other hand, used the place to prove her sexuality; she loved telling boys she was a stripper. Plus, she could pick up chicks there who would fuck her and whatever boy she happened to be dating. That stopped eventually, once one of her boyfriends bailed on her for a chick named Ruby they had fucked together one drug-induced night.

I, on the other hand, fucked indiscriminately in an entirely different way. I'd run into guys, trashed out of my mind, and picture them naked and grinding while knowing that I'd never want to speak with them. Not at all. I just needed to stop thinking about Adam, and fucking seemed like the way to do that.

One of the characters I used to provide orgasm-distraction was this Hollywood rock star I met on Sunset Strip.

Rick was the lead singer of this band that was very popular in Southern California, but in Southern California only. He wouldn't show me his pop rock band's videos, I guess he figured I'd laugh at how lame they were. Rick was one of those people I'd make fun of and still liked me enough to come back. He could take verbal assault, the poor guy. He was nice.

The first time Rick spoke to me was at the Rainbow. I was wearing a small black leather skirt and when he saw me going upstairs, he moved toward the railing and watched my legs all the way up. As I turned toward the bathroom, he hollered, "I'll be waiting for you in the hallway."

I pissed, thought about this guy I'd seen at the front door, reapplied red lipstick and I stepped out the bathroom door and into Rick, who I had forgotten about. But when I looked at him he had all of this long straight hair that seemed real enough and wasn't wearing acid-washed jeans. And there were girls all over him. A trio of blonds stood behind him giggling and a redhead pushed through them to ask for his autograph on a napkin. I couldn't understand why he was bothering with me. Probably because I had no interest. He followed me down to the bar, sat next to me and bought a couple double Jameson's. After we drank a bunch of whiskeys I told him, "I'm really not attracted to you. I really think you're a nice guy. And I like you, but you know."

I woke up the next morning naked in his huge bed. Damn.

So a couple nights later we attempted to go on a real dinner date, I told him I really wasn't into him again. We fucked again.

Then I met Eric. Bridget and I were down at this trendy bar on Melrose. She was draining bourbons and cokes, I was back on scotch and water. On about her third, she started to lean, and then suddenly jumped up onto the stool and stood there. "Check him out."

"What?"

"Him." She tapped me in the ribs with her foot and pointed. I grabbed her finger, pulled her down from the stool before the barkeep cut us off, and glanced over. There was this guy just nodding at this blathering woman beside him. He resembled somebody straight out of a Hollywood movie, a wax sculpture in motion.

"Go tell him I think he's hot," she said.

"What? That's stupid. You tell him." The barkeep dumped the melting ice cubes from my glass. They fell into the sink with a crash and a splatter. He dropped in new cubes, scotch, a squirt of water.

"I can't. I'm too drunk," Bridget said.

Jesus Christ, so was I, which was the only reason I went and did it. The chick next to him stopped talking when I moved up to the bar between them.

"My friend over there wants to fuck you." He looked into my eyes and then followed my gaze over to Bridget. She had lipstick on her teeth. The tag was sticking out of the back of her shirt. Her skirt was askew. She looked cute and drunk.

"What about you?"

"What about me?"

"Do you want to fuck me?"

"I don't know," he had me. "I think you're kind of too pretty for me. My friend over there, she digs you."

"Yeah, but I want to shove my cock inside of you."

I stood there looking at him for about a minute, trying to figure out how this happened. "Let's go," I said.

Eric had this two-bedroom apartment about a half-hour north of LA, in Canyon County. It was a new apartment and the only furniture he had wasn't furniture at all. It was a queen-sized egg carton-mattress and it lay, covered in some sheets, a comforter and a pile of blankets, on the floor.

The first night Eric brought me home he didn't even try anything. How odd. He surrounded the bathtub with candles and filled it with bubbles and hot water just for me. He even brought in a little radio he tuned to a classical music station. I felt weird. I wasn't used to being that clean and I wondered if he had some sort of bath fetish. Or maybe a clean fetish. It was kind of corny romantic but I sat in the hot tub, dehydrated, listening to Beethoven and thinking how nice Eric was. I must have passed out in that tub, because when I woke up it was morning and I was wearing Eric's thermal underwear and lying beside him on the floor under a pile of blankets.

The cool thing about Eric was, he really didn't know how perfect looking he was, so he wasn't an arrogant asshole about it. He grew up in northern Florida which made him far superior to LA natives. Had he been born in LA he would've been acutely aware of his looks, which would have ruined him completely.

He picked me up at my place and brought me to his every night for a week. Eric was newly divorced and he had this sweet doll-like two-year-old son he would videotape dancing around. We'd hang around taping his son until he went to sleep, and then drink and fuck. But after awhile I missed the bars. I missed the boys. We fizzled out.

Good timing anyway because Adam was back to play LA. He stopped at his apartment where he dumped some shit, gave me a call and then hiked over.

"Hey, open the fucking gate," I heard from below.

"There's no buzzer. Climb the fire escape."

"Oh fucking Jesus." But up he came, growling the entire climb. I ducked out my window to meet him and watched his face redden as he climbed the wrought iron ladder. When he reached the top, I could tell he was pissed about something. I tried to kiss him and he shoved me against the iron rail and climbed through the window. He reached into his jacket pocket and dug out a phone bill, shoved it in my face and pointed to the origin section of the calling card. Listed there was call after call from The Veil.

"What the fuck were you doing at The Veil?"

"Working." I touched his chest, he flinched.

"Working? Working? Is that what they call it?"

"Hey, find me a job and I'll take it. There are no fucking jobs around here and I need cash. What, do you want me to go on tour with you?" I had him there. I knew it was the last thing he wanted. Still, he was pissed. But he was always pissed. (Later, he wrote a song called "Death and the Devil," and said it was about that night with me. It was a love song, I guess.)

He tossed the bill on the floor, said he wasn't going to pay it, and pulled a smoke from behind his ear. He paced the tiny apartment, checking it out. We had only slept at his place.

It was a small dark studio, with a kitchen large

enough only for midget appliances and a tiny table. It was covered with a blue-flowered vinyl tablecloth from Target, which hid its plastic top, its plastic legs. It was a patio table I found on someone's patio. Or, as Bridget said, a found patio table.

The manager, this aspiring soap actor called Rudolpho, found me a sofa. Rudolpho had this raspy voice and choked on his spit every few words. He was entertaining—he always had me wondering if he'd cough to death in front of me.

"I got," he gagged, "a couch," he coughed, "for you." Rudolpho showed me a dirty white loveseat someone left in another apartment. He even carried it up two flights of stairs for me. I got a black coffee table from this guy Chris, who lived down the hall. He was one of the few tenants I actually knew and I only met him because we did laundry at the same time, 5 AM. We both prepared to sleep by smoking pot around that time. Then the pot had us doing laundry, which was a good thing. I had to clean my costumes some time. Whenever one of us would fall asleep and forget our laundry, the other would salvage it.

And when I didn't feel like playing with the rockers and drank at the Frolic Room on Hollywood, I'd see him there. Chris was a painter with thinning, shoulder-length hair, a blond goatee, ripped pants. I liked that his shoes were spattered and he always smelled of linseed oil. He was perfectly nice, but kind of boring. He spoke in monotone and didn't get excited about anything. Even his paintings were flat, and I wondered how he made any cash. Maybe all those boring Hollywood producers liked boring paintings.

But anyway he had this black coffee table he definitely didn't want. I liked how stupid it looked next to the stained white couch. Tacky. Maybe just poor. Hell, that's always been my look.

The only piece of furniture I actually bought was a double futon mattress and frame, but the frame was so cheap the wood continually split and I couldn't figure out how to get it in couch position. All it would do was recline or lie flat. Ah, well.

The walls were depressing, artless. I had nothing to cover the mold that grew during the rainy season, when a hole in the building's roof allowed water to stream down the walls. A torn pink patchwork comforter left over from childhood that I brought west with me hung over the double window, blocking the view of the sun drenched dumpster-filled alley. I was happy there.

"Nice place," Adam sardonically grinned.

"Well, you know."

He went into the bathroom and took a piss. I heard the hiss of the cigarette as it hit the toilet. He came back out and lay face up on the futon. I crawled on top of him. He was nearly a foot taller than me. I positioned my pelvis on top of his cock, and had to shift to reach up and kiss him. I closed my eyes and inhaled. He smelled vaguely like smoke, sweat, sex. Something sweet. Something comfortable. He smelled like Adam.

When we woke the next day, curled inside each

other, he reminded me he'd only had two nights in town and tonight was his last. After the show he'd get a few hours sleep and then hit the bus tomorrow morning. The band was again working its way up toward San Francisco, Portland, Seattle, Vancouver, before it flew out to Japan. I reached over, picked up the phone, and called in sick. Adam leaned over and found a pack of smokes on the floor, under his jeans. He shook one out, lit it, and laid back down. I turned on my side, facing him. He looked content—naked beside me on his back with tangled hair and a smoke. He lifted his chin to the ceiling as he exhaled.

"Hey, I've got something for you," he breathed out with a stream of smoke. I watched it disappear, and waited for the next.

"Yeah."

"Yeah. In my jacket pocket." I left the bed and picked up his black motorcycle jacket. He watched me pull out a Z T-shirt.

"I thought you could add it to your collection," he grinned. I ripped off my shredded Melvins T-shirt and pulled Adam over my head. The shirt had him sitting there, morose, with some porno chick positioned to go down on him. It made me laugh. He was so cool. I crawled back onto the hard thin futon.

"Thanks, baby." I put my head on his chest. I could hear his heart pounding, I could hear every breath. I laid my knee across his pelvis, cunt hairs rubbing against the side of his leg. He grabbed my knees, pulled my ass down toward him, and put his

face between my legs. His hair tickled as he tongue-
fucked me. I started laughing and pushed his head
away. When I caught my breath, he looked up at me,
red hair dancing on my skin as he climbed up to
kissed me. I tasted my pussy in his mouth. I reached
for his cock, guided it over to my pussy, slid it in
and gasped. I could feel him grinning. "Missed me,
huh, baby."

Oh yeah. I did.

4

I missed that. I missed Adam, which is the only reason I went to the Whiskey with Bridget the night he finally came back to town. It was the only reason I was now standing on Adam's doorstep. I tried the door. Locked. But I figured it would be when I left his show, and had also figured a way around it. I walked over to the side of the building, the heels of my fuck-me boots sinking into the grass, into the dirt. The latch on Adam's bedroom window never worked and I knew he would never bother to fix it. When I ripped off the screen, I tripped over what I could only figure was a giant root wedged behind my heel and fell over into a bush, scraping my thighs, scraping my boots. After pulling twigs out from under my skirt, out of my hair and righting myself, I reached out to shove the window up. It stuck. It probably hadn't been opened since I lived there. It took me a couple good pushes to get the thing up. I hiked my skirt up to my waist and crawled boot-first into the window, crushing my tits on the way in. I sat on the bed, pulled off my boots and looked at the damage. Not bad on the boots, not bad on the legs. Not too much blood.

I stretched out on Adam's bed and pulled up the covers. When I rolled over I heard a crunch. I rummaged through the sheets and found a torn-open, empty Trojan wrapper in the bed. Fucking slut, I thought, tossing it to the floor.

I heard the door open and scuffing feet. Then came Adam's indistinguishable gruff laugh and a giggle. A fucking giggle! The bastard brought a chick home. I bounced off the bed and into the living room.

Adam froze when he saw me.

"What the fuck are you doing here?"

"No, you fuckhead," I screamed, pulling our wedding ring off my finger. I threw it at him. It bounced off his forehead. He blinked. "We're married, you fuck! Who the hell is this cunt and anyway how could you even *think* of fucking such an ugly bitch!"

And she was an ugly bitch. She had lank brown hair, googley eyes, a fully pierced face and a huge ass. A nice ass. I was jealous because I knew Adam loved big butts. Still, though, the ass thing wasn't enough. Not for Adam.

"Since when are you into face piercings?" I taunted. "Hell, I'd understand maybe if the holes were larger and provided some face-fucking value. Or do they stretch?"

That really pissed Adam off—his face turned bright red, something he hated, being a red-head and all.

"You bitch," he quietly hissed at me.

"You," I pointed at the chick. "You get the fuck out of here."

I was surprised at the balls on that chick: she wouldn't budge. She probably figured it was her big chance to fuck a rock star. Or maybe she was a plaster caster. Fucking freak.

"She's not going anywhere. You are."

"I am? You want to fuck that thing? What is that about?"

"If you don't leave I'm going to call the cops."

"Call the fucking cops, you dick." I went back into his room and opened his top drawer. Yup. There it all was. All of my stuff: short stories, pictures, switch-blade, play bills, the Gauguin catalogue. I started stacking everything into a pile atop the dresser except for the knife which I dropped into one of my boots. I ripped a flattened pillow out of its case and threw all evidence of me in there—my underwear, a dried black rose I had given him—the job almost complete when I heard the cops at the door. What the fuck. The LAPD arriving in a timely manner. Or maybe it was still speed-time. I decided it wouldn't be good to be charged with robbery on top of every-thing else and so I dropped the pillowcase, grabbed my boots and jumped, bare-footed, bare-legged, out the window. I steadied myself, managed to avoid the bush and ran as fast as I could through the yard next door and the yard beyond that. I remembered that the next street over had a skuzzy alley attached to it that anyone in their right mind, and the cops, knew not to go into. I had found my destination.

Ann Wood

When I reached the street, I ran blindly across and nearly into an oncoming SUV which slammed on its breaks—the screech informing the cops as to my whereabouts. I skidded into the alley and crouched behind a filthy green dumpster that smelled of fish and piss. My feet stuck to the concrete below but my pupils were too small to see in the dark and I couldn't tell what the sticky stuff might be.

A few minutes later I saw the pair of uniformed cops standing across the street, talking about what they should do. One of them stomped over to the alley entrance with his flashlight and shined its beam inside. He was so round he couldn't bend down. I crouched as low as I could.

"Let's just go back to the car," he huffed. His partner had this swagger that reminded me of Eddie in the film *Barfly*, tough and stupid at the same time. He grunted and back they went.

Then I felt movement beside me. My eyes finally adjusted to the darkness and I saw the shape of a man lying on the ground. A needle hung out of his arm and blood oozed out. Well, at least he was moving. That was a good sign.

I bolted from the alley and headed up the road, away from the cops. I slowed to a walk and kept moving until I reached Sunset Boulevard, until I reached Rock 'n' Roll Denny's.

When I got there I figured I must look a mess so I pushed through the after-hours crowd collectively waiting for a table and ran into the bathroom. Some chicks stood in the middle of the bathroom, reapplying lipstick. I looked past them into the stained, cracked mirror and saw a flushed face but, aside from that, I didn't look so bad after all. My hair was a mess but hey, I could've just been fucked rather than chased. I went into a stall to take a leak and put on my boots.

When I came out I heard someone calling my name. It was that freak Jimmy.

I met him at Boardners one drunken night long ago and went to his house, fucked him and passed out. I awoke to a ringing phone, he rolled over and answered it.

"What the fuck are you calling so early for? It's only goddamn nine o'clock. . . . I don't fucking care if the hospital's about to discharge you, you know the fucking rule. . . . Take a fucking cab. . . . No, and don't call me again." He slammed down the receiver and rolled back onto his potbelly.

"Who was that?"

"My Dad."

Yikes. When he fell back asleep, I escaped.

So there he was, the freak that left his pop in the hospital. But he had a car and he didn't know Adam. He could drive me home, I figured, it really wasn't too far out of his way. So I went over to the table.

"Hey, here, sit down here. What's going on? I haven't seen you in awhile," the glutton said, chomping on some third-rate steak and eggs.

"Yeah, well, you know Jimmy. Work and all that. Hey, any chance you'd give me a lift? I sort of lost my ride."

"Sure baby, whatever you want. Whatever you want."

He and these dudes jabbered on nonsensically and gobbled down their food. When Jimmy finished he threw a twenty down on the table, said "Later," and we headed out to his Mercedes. I had forgotten about that. A fucking Mercedes. What a punk. He drove down Sunset but rather than turning left on Highland, he took a right.

"Hey, man, where're you going? I thought you said you'd bring me home."

"No, baby, we're going to my place." He reached over and put his cold, chubby palm on my thigh. It felt like a frog landed on my leg, but stickier. I pushed it away.

"The fuck we are. I need to get home."

"What?"

"I said, motherfucker, take me home."

He slammed on the breaks—I slammed into the dashboard. Jimmy leaned over me and pushed the door open. He pressed his wet palms against me and shoved.

"Hey, what the fuck? You said you'd give me a ride," I said, trying to maintain my position in the passenger seat.

"Get the fuck out!"

I resisted, realized it was useless, and remembered my switchblade. My right hand gripped the door handle and kept me in place while my left pulled the knife from my boot. As Jimmy continued pushing on me, I pressed the little metal button down and the sharp blade sprang from its shield. With one swoop I jabbed him in the thigh. He screeched like a pig in a slaughter house. When he pressed both hands against his leg to try and stop the blood from spurting out, I dropped out onto the pavement and ripped open my knee. The car sped off with a wide-open passenger door.

I hoped he'd get car-jacked.

I hoped I hit a giant vein.

Fucking pussy.

I hiked up the hill toward Hollywood and once I hit the boulevard all sorts of cars began pulling over as I walked by, waiting for me to walk up, make a deal, get inside. A white limo stopped ahead of me block after block. I just kept moving.

Once I passed the Chinese Theater I noticed a gang of big black guys that were either drug dealers, pimps, or both. They looked like they had just popped out of a music video, but I didn't see Ice Cube anywhere. One of them wore a black pinstripe suit with white cowboy boots and a feathered fedora. Another had a bandana tied like a sweatband around his head and wore a tank top, tight jeans and Pumas. They all wore at least two heavy gold chains and lots of cologne—I could smell them through the stench of exhaust. I looked behind me and saw a cop car. I headed toward the gang.

"Hey, what's happening," I said as I walked by. They nodded in appreciation. We were the same: stylish degenerates working the town.

Then came the blue flashing lights as a cruiser pulled up to the curb beside me. I kept walking as the hustlers surrounded the cop car. "Whattda-ya want boys," they heckled in unison as I limped away.

I climbed the fire escape and into my apartment where I washed the blood off my legs and realized I'd never be able to sleep. I couldn't stop thinking about Adam. After all the shit we'd been through I couldn't believe it was over because I missed one fucking plane.

It happened about four months ago. I hadn't heard from Adam in a couple weeks. I was flying high on speed when the phone rang.

"Hey baby."

It took me a few seconds to realize who it was. "Adam."

"Yeah baby. Cancel everything. Today's my birthday and we got a week off. I got you a plane ticket so you can meet me in Hawaii. It's waiting for you at the airport. Like a honeymoon, you know. I know you think that's corny shit but we'll be alone for five nights. The thing is, you've got to get to LAX right now. The flight leaves in two hours."

"I'll be there," I said, but thought, two fucking hours. Typical Adam, turning our honeymoon into a challenge. Always testing, to see if I'd abandon him like his mother did.

"I love you baby. See you in a few." He hung up.

I did not want to miss that plane. I decided not to waste any time and didn't bother to pack. I looked in my bag and saw that I had enough cash for a cab and a couple drinks on the plane. Fuck the strip club. Girls went MOA all the time. I grabbed my boots, sat on the futon to put them on and wondered how Adam's mom could leave him like that.

I hated that story about his mother. She and his

father were matched up in church. Not a normal church—if there is such a place—but some Christian revivalist cult-like church. Maybe it was a cult. I couldn't tell from the stories he told, but Adam was pretty fucked up so it probably was. Anyway, his mother was something like seventeen when she was married off to this 45-year-old Christian. Adam was born ten months later. Things were OK for a few years, I guess. Then, when Adam was about four, his mother finally snapped and disappeared. His father didn't seem to mind. He married a different Christian, had more kids, and life went on. Adam never heard from his mother again. He was still mad at her for leaving him with the cult Christians. He was obsessed with being abandoned, he talked about it all the time. And when we first met he would purposely be a dick to see if I'd leave him, but I was mostly too drunk to notice anyhow.

When I got my boots laced up tight I looked at the clock. I had been thinking about Adam's mother and tying my boots for ninety minutes. I couldn't see how that happened. I'd never make it now. Fucking speed.

I had no Hawaiian number to call. I didn't know where Adam was staying. I didn't know what to do so I snorted another line of speed and went out into the night. I never heard from Adam again.

And now Adam and that pierced chick were swimming through my head. He was probably fucking her and there was nothing I could do about it. My ring finger felt bare. I needed some sleep. My body ached, my mind ached. I rifled through my bathroom drawers for some weed, but all I found was a few lines of snort and a big unopened box of tampons. I thought about using a tampon applicator as an inhaler and decided it wouldn't work. I rolled up a crisp dollar, shoved it up my nose and snorted. Half-feeling the smooth grain of cocaine entangled in nostril hairs, I snorted again. I looked in the mirror. Clean face. I wasn't really feeling it yet, so I snorted some water to speed it up. I could taste the diluted coke as it dripped down and burned the back of my throat. My mind started jittering but my hands weren't shaking. Then I started thinking about that box of tampons. Unopened. Purchased months ago. Holy shit, I figured I must be pregnant.

The first thing I thought about this was, well, how can I not have this baby? I worried about blowing my chance. I would tell Adam, maybe he'd be OK with it and we could take care of it together. Assuming it was his, but even if it wasn't. But how could it not be his, my coked-up mind rattled, it has to be Adam's. I could just picture its soft pudgy body and round head covered in orange fuzz.

I started feeling sick.

I took off my clothes and curled up in a blanket on top of the futon. I listened to my mind scream and waited for it to shut the fuck up.

It was light out when I came to. I dragged my eye to the clock. It read something like seven, maybe eight. It was too early. I was barely conscious. I was barely alive. I fell back into a thoughtless, dreamless slumber.

Bolt Risk

An hour later there was a pounding on the door.

I was trying to clear my head, shake the noise into my brain. My first thought was of that poor girl, pounding on Parris's door. The second was that I was naked. The noise continued, and then a loud voice shouted through the door, "Open up in there. This is the police."

The police? I figured they had the wrong apartment. I pulled my thin blanket tightly around me and hobbled over to the door. There was no peephole. I opened the door. A cop shoved me aside and three others ran in, casing the place. The cop who pushed me said, "Get your clothes on."

"What? You've got no fucking right."

"Get your clothes on," another shove, down went the blanket. "You're under arrest."

My brain started screaming. My mouth started screaming. I was standing there, naked and screaming.

This chick cop grabbed the Z T-shirt and a pair of jeans off the floor and threw them at me, "Put these on. We're taking you in with or without clothes."

I put them on. The pants were tight in the belly, loose at the waist, denim bunched from knee-to-ankle. They were Adam's. The cop who shoved me cuffed my wrists. I was left shoeless like Charlie Manson and shoved into the backseat of a police car.

At the station, the cops grabbed my hands and blackened my fingertips with ink, individually pressing each against a long, stiff strip of paper. Marked on the strips were two-word phrases typed in miniature print: right ring, left thumb. Then came the mug shots for which I held up both stained middle fingers and grinned manically. I thought it'd be funny if it ever hit the stands. Some chick cop with a large heart-shaped mole on her right cheek grabbed some shackles. She locked them around my wrists, around my ankles. The chain that connected the two sets wound about me like a metal snake. She and this boy cop with a military haircut were laughing about something. I wished I were in on the fun.

I was returned to the caged backseat of the police car and delivered to the courthouse in silence. My brain was still thinking it was all a big mistake and I'd be sent home soon enough. I decided the judicial system must work, after all isn't this *Free to Be You and Me* America? You know, all that civil rights shit we were taught we had growing up in the 1970s. It amazed me that Marlo Thomas jumped on that shit. She became Ms. Women's Rights but got herself a nose job—that's how good she felt about it all. Never posed in Playboy either. At least I don't think she did.

I marched by the metal detectors, the guards, the lawyers, the guilty and the not-so-guilty in the courthouse. I marched into the basement. There were a dozen cells in a row and as I walked by the other prisoners I heard hisses, I heard cat calls.

"Hey, you're a pretty one. I'd like to eat your cunt," some decrepit old woman pronounced.

"She looks like a bad girl who needs a whippin' to me," another crusty one growled. I felt an irrepressible sigh escape me.

I sat in that cold, windowless cell for hours; unable to gauge the hour or temperature of the day. As the morning droned on, some guy called in an order of lunch meat sandwiches. Delivered quickly, they looked like they came out of a vending machine. The sandwiches hissed and sagged when the plastic tops were pulled off, so they probably did. I watched the inmates next door scoffing them down. The guy who phoned in the order was annoyed that I asked for a smoke rather than a sandwich, but passed me one anyhow.

I was beginning to get chilly when the court appointed psychologist strolled up to my cell. His nose was wide and browner than the rest of his face. His forehead was slick. Sweaty papers were clutched in his puffy palms. Adam's cramped handwriting filled a page.

I went to the back of the cage and sat on the floor; I could feel the cold concrete through my jeans. The psychologist was so sweaty that I silently wondered if he was coming down off some drugs. I feared that he'd raise his pits and I'd see dust clinging to wet stench, but he kept his arms close, guarded. He stayed far enough away to protect himself from me and the air remained that dusty sort of scentless.

"Hey, man, I didn't ask for you. I need a lawyer."

"It doesn't work that way, missy, when you're on the verge being committed to a psychiatric hospital."

"What the fuck are you talking about? These cops shove their way into my apartment while I'm sleeping and arrest me without reason, shackle me and now you're committing me to a mental hospital? What about my civil rights? What about my one phone call?"

"Listen, you're going away for your own good. Your husband here says you've threatened to kill him and yourself."

"What? If I wanted him dead, he'd be dead. And anyhow, we don't live together."

He started scribbling stuff down. Aw, shit, my speech never was cognitively conceived. But then I made my points: I'm not suicidal, there's no evidence that I've ever been suicidal, Adam's just mad at me, I never threatened him, we don't live together, I've got to go to work.

The psychologist scrunched his bloated face. "This is serious, and you better take it seriously, missy. The fact that you were allowed to live with neurosis for so long is, quite frankly, worrisome." As he walked away he said, "Your father says that you withdraw from social interaction, which is a symptom of schizophrenia. He says you've never been able to get along in society and are growing more isolated as you grow older. That's a sure sign of acute mental illness." He was still talking as he walked down the hallway and out the door.

My father? How could that be? Well, this guy apparently knew nothing. Nothing about my family, nothing about my psychology. I figured the judge couldn't take him seriously. He had no evidence. Nothing.

But that quack was more powerful than I supposed. He stood in court and blandly said he spoke with Adam and my father and examined me. Nice examination, I thought, low standards. He said that I worked as a prostitute and had recent drug and alcohol related arrests. Well, I thought, it's true that I find prostitution in the Red Light District of Amsterdam amusing, but not enough to actually work it, or LA. He said that I was suicidal and threatened to kill my husband. Somehow he missed about every justifiable reason to commit me, my brain laughed. When he said I should be hospitalized, I was reminded of why I didn't go to graduate school: I didn't want to be one of those useless people with several degrees.

The judge turned to the court appointed lawyer. "Do you have something to say in defense?"

The guy in the shiny, anti-wrinkle suit barely stood up. He was so sullen he reminded me of an undertaker, but less interesting. After all, he'd never embalmed anybody. When I spoke to him earlier that day I actually asked him if he was an undertaker, and he embarrassedly admitted that he grew up in the apartment above his father's funeral home. We talked about that for a couple minutes and then he asked me if I'd ever been hospitalized. That was it. Now he was standing in my defense.

"No, your honor. I have nothing to say," said the lawyer, falling limply to his seat. And I thought, he should've followed in his father's footsteps after all.

Then I noticed Adam standing across the room, behind armed guards, behind a banister. When the judge announced my commitment, Adam lifted his chin and I recognized that arrogant posture of disdain. Fuck him, I'd remain unaffected. I thought I could handle that until I saw my father standing next to him. I didn't know that they even knew each other. But there they were, the two self-centered men I spent a lifetime simultaneously running away from and chasing. They joined together to lock me up. I was frightened and flattered. They were expressionless, cold. I couldn't stand to look at either one of them.

I turned my eyes to the yellow plaster ceiling. The shackles made this metal-on-metal grating noise, as shrill as fingernails on chalkboard. The sound screeched through the courtroom. Everyone winced. It reminded me of the time Adam tried to teach me to play guitar. He was patient until I fucked up "Iron Man" for the third time, then he nearly lost it. I couldn't blame him. I sucked. My fingers didn't work that way. And anyhow it was the same reaction I got from my father when I attempted to perform one of Helena's monologues in *A Midsummer Night's Dream.*

A pair of court officers stood up. One grabbed my elbow. The other grabbed my other elbow.

"Excuse me your honor," I said. "Can I say something in my own defense?"

I actually thought he would let me. Instead, he waived his hand in the air, casting me off. The court officers pulled me away, muttering to my protests that it wasn't permanent.

Still shackled, I sat in my own cage in the van like a lion traveling to its next circus show. A bunch of men heading to the house of corrections were in the van too, but they got to share a separate cage. I figured it'd be more fun in there. I wanted to ask those fellows down back what they were in for.

Bolt Risk

Probably they would have repeated the usual, each would've said his cunt-of-a-wife had him captured so she could fuck her boyfriend. She was pissed because he got drunk and beat the shit out of her, they would say. But hearing it aloud would have amused me, even if only temporarily. It would have put my mind on something other than my own brain.

"Wow, that was something back there in court," the driver, who was the first court officer to grab my elbow, whistled through his teeth. "Didn't know it was so easy to commit someone."

I was startled. "Yeah, how come I couldn't even say anything?"

The driver whistled the sound of a diving bomb.

I left it at that.

After dropping everyone else at the county jail, I was driven over to the psychiatric hospital. It looked like a modern-day Dachau. In fact, it looked almost exactly like Jourhaus, the entrance building. Two large metal doors hung dead center, two sets of barred double windows flanking either side, with five smaller windows lined up across the top. There were no flowers, no bushes, nothing but a large paved parking lot and two skinny trees that stood by the road. If you did escape, there was no immediate place to hide.

I always knew I'd end up locked in Dachau. It was just a matter of time.

"Do you want me to take your shackles off here, before you get inside?" the whistling officer wanted to know.

"No. I'd rather walk in this way. It'll scare the normals."

He laughed in agreement and walked me to the large metal doors. Posted on one were two words: Bolt Risk. There was a buzz and they opened to two attendants dressed all in white. I rattled my way past them, feeling the ghostly sensation of being neither alive nor dead.

Pressed against the wall at the entrance of the ward was this balding underground artist I vaguely knew as Sew, looking good and drugged up. Lucky him. Across from him stood a young guy with shaggy blond hair I figured was a musician. He looked angry the way only a teenager can—glowing with pure hatred for no reason, nor reason for a reason. The attendants pulled me down the hall. The one on the left pressed me into the black plastic chair positioned in front of the open window where medications were dispensed in tiny paper ketchup cups. It made me think of Burger King, it made me wish I had some fries.

Whistler bent down and began unlocking my ankles with his key. Then came the wrists. "Bye." He walked off. As he left, he whistled something that reminded me of Mozart's String Quintet in G Minor Menuetto, it was so sadly hopeful.

After the mundane—the nurse slapping on the hospital bracelet, my stepping on a scale, the nurse drawing blood, my peeing in a cup, my answering a thousand simplistic questions, the nurse saying, "Here's what you're swallowing for meds, here's your room, that's your roommate,"—I went into the television room. The nurse told me there's no way I could get out until the psychiatrist came in the morning anyway.

The wooden couch wobbled as if stuck together with glue. I fell back on some brown itchy cushions that smelled like rotting socks. The television was turned to some generic sitcom but the drugs were kicking in and it was better then lying in the bed next to my roommate, a 400-pound woman whose snore, I was told, could be heard ward-wide.

Cynthia's entire body was comprised of one giant roll of blubber after another. Her neck looked like an inflated donut-shaped water float. She smoked incessantly, she told me, but was new to the joint and didn't have smoking privileges yet. Nor could she handle going cold turkey. All she wanted was her nicotine fix.

Sympathetic, her husband secretly passed her a pack of smokes and a lighter during visitation hour that afternoon and so after the check nurse made her usual five-minute round, Cynthia would go into the bathroom, stand on the toilet seat and blow smoke directly into the fan. I joined her a couple of times, but it was impossible to squeeze into the bathroom with her, which turned out to be a lucky thing for me. I guess the fan didn't work so well, because they caught Cynthia smoking on her fifth go around.

"Where are the matches? Where is the lighter? It must be turned over immediately or there will be consequences!"

When Cynthia refused, the staff began its search.

They tore apart our room—every drawer, every pocket, every corner was examined.

When they came up empty handed, it was cavity search time.

Cynthia was taken off by the cavity searchers. I figured I had a lot of time to myself, Cynthia had a lot of cavities. I lay quietly on my appointed mattress visualizing a group of nurses using tongs to individually unfold each ripple of fat and finding dirt, fuzz, food, a sickening stench. The smell so overwhelming that I imagine a young nurse running from the room, puking.

As it turned out, she stashed the lighter in her cunt. That's where the searchers found it. I didn't want to picture that at all.

Cynthia was sent to isolation before bedtime. I was glad not to hear her snoring and so, I think, was the rest of the ward.

She was still in isolation when I met Ryan the next day. It turned out the parents of this shaggy-haired teen had him committed because they hated his friends, his band, his drug use. He told me that two weeks ago, the day after his sixteenth birthday, he was arrested and committed to the institution. Same story, different scene.

Ryan was impressed that Adam had me committed because he liked Z a lot. He asked me questions about tunings and pedals, I knew half the answers. He was cute and liked talking about music. And he had these friends who brought him coke every day during visitors hours. We'd snort it together. So it took getting committed to a psych hospital to find a constant coke supply in Hollywood. I guess I was hanging in the wrong circles.

That night, I dreamed Adam was screaming at me in the hospital. He was standing over where I was lying curled in a fetal position. Even in the dream the sheets were stiff and cold and the pillow smelled of Lysol which permeated the air ward-wide. I wanted my pillow, the one I pressed my face against night after night. The one that lay on my futon, covered in make-up stains and drool. The one that smelled like my mother's shoulder.

Then, suddenly, there she was. My mother. My mother who'd been dead since I was five. She had aged appropriately, she looked about as old as my father. She was still beautiful. She still had MS. She was still reading books.

"Don't worry," she said, petting my head. "It's all a good story. Death is the ultimate story, but you can't write it down."

She faded away and Adam was standing there shouting again. He shouted about what I should do, how I should be. He shouted about how I shouldn't be me. I couldn't understand it. Adam was the one person who I thought actually liked me for being real. But it wasn't what he wanted at all. He wanted compliance. How boring-typical. How obvious.

My leg jerked in response and I woke up, the stiff sheets wet with sweat. I walked blindly into the florescent hallway and toward the nurses' station to get a new pair of green hospital wear. The nurse gave me that and a Xanax. I downed the pill.

What woke me in the morning was the check nurse standing over me with her clipboard hollering, "Check! Wake up! Med time." I half fell out of bed and crawled into the bathroom to take a piss. My mind pounded after me. Out in the hallway in paper slippers, I stood in line behind this group of characters—a woman with a red greasy face and pointed nose that formed a V; a perfectly made-up housewife in a leotard and matching pink sweatbands; a fat man in an old tattered robe with a banana sticking out of the pocket. I stood right behind the banana guy. He smelled rank, like rotted fruit. His name was Fred, he said, and asked if I'd ever smoked a banana peel.

"A banana peel?"

"Yeah, people say you can dry them up, smoke them, and get high."

"Does it work?"

"A little bit. It's not as good as pot, though. Hey Walter, over here."

Walter was thin with sagging sallow flesh, as if he'd been deflated long ago. In his flannel shirt was a pocket protector which held a couple pens. He wore loose jeans and sweat socks. I kept waiting for his pants to slide off.

"This is Walter. He is also drying banana peels."

"Really. Good to meet you Walter."

Walter squeaked and held out his hand. They were funny. I decided I'd sit with them at breakfast.

At medication time, Fred swallowed three pills, Walter two, and I had five. I wondered what that meant. The nurses made me lift my tongue to ensure

Bolt Risk

I wasn't hiding pills, which I thought odd, the drugs probably the best thing about the joint.

At breakfast time, Fred and Walter showed me where to pull my tray from the cart. On it was decaffeinated tea, canned fruit in a plastic dish and a carton of milk. I had just set it down on a table when the red-faced woman started screaming, "That's not ketchup. It's blood. Stop the stabbing! Daddy, stop the stabbing!" An orderly rushed over. He stopped when he saw what she'd done. The screamer used a plastic fork to tear off the skin on her wrist and was stabbing at her veins with the utensil. It was rather savage—there was a lot of blood, broken plastic, shredded skin. I decided to skip breakfast and return my tray to the stand.

A nurse stopped me in the hallway and directed me into an office. She opened my file and put a form and a pen in front of me.

"We'd like you to sign this. It just says that you're here voluntarily."

I looked at the piece of paper. It was a voluntary commitment form. "I'm not signing this. I want to get out of here."

"Well, it's possible that we'll think you are a rational person if you sign this, and it only says you volunteer for thirty days. You're committed anyway."

"Hey, I already read this book." I stood up, walked out and went directly to the pay phone, where I dialed Adam's number. Voicemail. "Adam. It's me. I don't know what's going on here and I need to talk to you. Really it's I need some of my stuff." My throat started closing in on me, I felt a heave escape.

I hung up fast. Someone was behind me. That check nurse again.

"Check. It's group therapy time. You're in Group B. You're there," She pointed to the stinky couch room. I doubted that meant we'd be zoning out on television. As it turned out, staff spent all this time trying to teach us something like Life 101. They tried to teach us conformity, how to play nice, how to behave in society. Or something like that. All I know is that the therapists wanted to end Ryan's sex fixation, Walter's banana fixation and everything about me. Even if they couldn't name exactly what it was.

Walter, the pink leotard woman, the underground artist and Ryan were all in Group B. We sat around talking about dried banana peels when this dyed-blond psychologist with big hair, big tits and sharp red nails walked in.

"My name is Dr. Sandwich and this is group therapy where we share our deepest feelings and thoughts about ourselves," she said. "Without judgment."

"And what is your deepest darkest feeling Dr. Sandwich," Ryan said, a little spark shot through bloodshot eyes.

"Now, Ryan, don't be fresh. Why don't we go around the room and tell about ourselves."

Linda in the leotard breathed her name quietly. "I don't," she huffed, "wanna talk." Walter squeaked that he had many projects to attend to upon release, and Ryan told the psychologist that he liked her tits. She was unmoved. Then she looked at me. I said I felt my experience mirror Kafka's *The Trial*. Her brow wrinkled; she was confused. When I told her the story of *The Trial*—how Joseph K. was accused of an unnamed crime he knew nothing about, how he was repeatedly sent to some strange courtroom in a tenement—and pointed out vague similarities to my own commitment, she said it sounded familiar. She maybe had read part of it. No one else had read the book. No one else said anything, but the underground artist.

"This is all inspiration. Progressing through the block, nothing more," Sew said.

"Well," Dr. Sandwich cleared her throat and her breasts heaved. Heaving breasts, I thought, I didn't know it was possible, really. She looked at me. Did I speak aloud? Then I saw what she was looking at, my hands. They were shaking, hard. My mind was racing, fast. Faster than it ever did on speed. I couldn't stop thinking about heaving breasts which lead to amputations, missing legs, the grotesque, Harry Crews, Flannery O'Connor, famous writers no one around here had even heard of. I got up and walked out to the nurses station, presented my shaking hands to a disinterested uniform.

"Oh, that's just a side effect of the lithium. It might go away."

"Lithium? I haven't even seen a doctor yet."

"Oh, well, you will today. Have a Xanax."

I sat on my hands for the rest of the morning, but my brain wouldn't stop vibrating.

After lunch I tried calling Adam again. He wasn't answering his phone. Voicemail, again. I left a stupid message, again. Then I felt someone behind me. I turned and saw an Asian doctor leering at me. He smelled like scallions.

"Come with me," he said from behind his foggy glasses. "I'm your psychiatrist, Dr. Chan."

I hung up the phone and followed. Inside Dr. Chan's professional office was a large mahogany desk, a chest and three plush chairs. I fell into a chair and sighed, body motionless except for my hands.

"Well," he said, flipping through my chart and eyeing me simultaneously. "I don't know why you're here. No episodes I can see. Why don't you tell me what's going on."

"I don't know. There's no reason for me to be here."

"No, the court makes commitments for reasons," he shuffled through some more pages. "Ah, here's one, you're suicidal."

"Um, no, I'm not."

"You may not feel suicidal, but that doesn't mean you are not suicidal," he said.

"I'm not even depressed."

"You're not depressed at this moment because you are now experiencing mania and that, too, is a serious illness."

"What? You're saying I'm manic depressive?"

"We prefer to call it bipolar disorder. But you're a beautiful woman. You can recover. You need only follow our treatment program and you'll be a fine, fine woman." He stood up and leaned against the front of his desk. His legs pressed against mine. "But you must eat, you don't want to get too thin.

Now I will see another patient."

I walked into the hallway, nauseated. How'd he figure I'd eat after that display? I wondered if Fred had any dried bananas I could smoke.

Art therapy was better. I found some clay that wasn't completely dried up and made figures and faces. Naked, disfigured figures. Creepy, evil faces.

A white coat came in to retrieve me from my monster-making. I noticed her little wispy mustache when she sat behind her desk. Her desktop was clear but for a clean blotter and framed photograph of an Alaskan Husky wearing a cowboy hat and bandana.

Amy, that's what she said her name was, decided that I was a closet homosexual and depressed about it.

"Why don't you want your husband? Why would you leave your husband? Why kill your husband? Because society has imposed him on you! You are angry, confused. You need to come out as a lesbian."

"I'm hardly married."

"Denial! It's the ultimate indicator. You must deny your marriage as you deny your sexual preference. You are at a crossroads, you are becoming a woman."

"Listen, I don't care either way but I fuck way too many boys to be a lesbian." I used as much energy as I could muster to stand.

"Boys! Exactly! Never refer to them as men. They are not men," she said as I staggered away.

I went to the window and asked for Xanax. A

frightened little nurse asked how many I'd like, and passed them over. I thought about how easy it would be to take the keys away from her and bolt. It had its possibilities.

The next psychologist wore round, wire rimmed glasses and a tweed sports coat complete with suede patches on the elbows. He was attached to whatever kind of herbal tea the time of day allowed. When he sat across from me with his Lemon Zinger, I could see that cognitive-behavioral-therapy-theory twirling around in his brain: change the thoughts, change the behavior, change them both. A non-surgical lobotomy. I sat there, trying to convince him nothing was wrong. That I ought not be there. He sat there, unmoved.

"You're hiding something," he nudged, "What is it?"

"There's nothing there, man." He grinned when I said "man." I decided I'd try "dude" soon. "I'd be happy to rap with you about things, but there's nothing wrong with my life."

He looked disappointed. I couldn't tell whether it was because I used the word "rap" or because he knew I was a stripper and refused to relay any good pornography. One could never tell.

Another chick therapist decided the problem was alcohol and drugs.

"Look, you're doing a lot of drugs and drinking heavily. It's messing with your mind," she said, tapping a pencil against my thickening chart.

"Yeah, I could probably agree but who cares. Substance control is a form of behavioral psychology and if you think that changing my behavior would change anything, you don't know much. That's ridiculously simplistic," I thought aloud.

"The court committed you for a reason," the therapist responded. "There's something going on."

She was the end of the line. There were no more therapists; all failed in having me voluntarily commit to the hospital, all failed in getting the story.

I failed in getting released.

The next morning I realized powerlessness. It hit me like a thud to the chest.

I was sitting at breakfast, behind a muffin and a pat of margarine stuck between a wax paper and cardboard square. In the red plastic mug a bloated decaf tea bag floated in luke-warm water. It smelled like coffee. My tongue tasted warm plastic liquid. I found a plastic knife sitting under the red plastic plate. I slid the knife down my pants and dumped the tray.

I stood in the hall. The checker walked by me and said "check." When I heard that dry tears cracked from the corners of my eyes and I booked to the bathroom. I locked the door and moisture surfaced. I became a bawling, heaving mess.

I took the plastic knife to my hair and sawed at it—a few strands at a time. The knife split the ends as I sawed as close to my scalp as I could. Hair filled the sink, hair fell on my feet.

I was screaming, I realized, when the checker started banging on the door. There was no escape. There was no where to go. I squeezed my body between the sterile sink and toilet. Lysol invaded my nose. Someone was fumbling with the door, fumbling with the lock. The bathroom door crashed open.

Four nurses came in hollering. One hollered with a needle. One hollered with restraints, one with a tourniquet, the other to 'Get down!' The last one shoved me against the toilet, the first shot me up with something, the second pulled the rubber from my upper arm, the third tied the restraints, the fourth wouldn't let me go.

My muscles became mush and I was pulled from under the sink. My body slid forward. My vision was foggy. I felt like I had opened my eyes underwater in an over-chlorinated pool—everything in the hallway rippled, my eyes burned. I watched unidentifiable figures move in slow motion as I was dragged down the hall and locked in a padded room.

It reminded me of a gym. Green mats that smelled like sweat, socks and piss covered the floor and walls. Monster eyes periodically peered through the tiny mesh and glass window in the door and watched me. My brain couldn't think of how to move my arms or legs. My brain couldn't think at all.

Time must have passed because at some point I was able to direct my body to the corner of the room closest to the door so those monsters couldn't see me. I could feel my wet underwear, my wet hospital drawers. At some point I had pissed myself. I was contemplating this when Dr. Chan showed up. I begged him to listen to me.

"I'm fucking powerless. I shouldn't be here. I'm locked up without just cause."

Bolt Risk

The tears wouldn't let up. My eyes burned. I felt my face puff up and I wanted to puke. He looked at me and quietly said that if I didn't relax, they'd never release me. They'd have proof I belonged there. I'd just have to wait out this stay, he said.

"And then, you can always live in my house with me. It is a very big house, it used to be a guest house, where former patients stay from time to time. They are good girls, like you could be."

He told me he'd release me from isolation but I'd have to clean up and behave.

I slunk out into the ward to wash up, down some more Xanax and snort some more coke.

Dr. Chan woke me from a drug-induced slumber that night and led me out of the ward and down into the basement. I didn't feel awake. I didn't feel asleep. I couldn't tell the difference, really. Everything was hazy. I wondered aloud if my mother was still here. Chan didn't respond. We walked into a pale green room that could have been any hospital room except that there were no magazines, no newspapers, no windows. Nothing but a couple of metal chairs shoved against the far wall, a table with protruding stirrups, a small machine and some tools reminiscent of that movie where Jeremy Irons played identical twin doctors who jammed sick gynecological shit up the cunts of unsuspecting patients.

"Your history of drug use coupled with the medications we require are harming the fetus. It's best that it be removed," Dr. Chan said, patting my stomach.

Ann Wood

"You're going to give me an abortion?"

He grinned. His smile was as big as a clown's. But toothier. "Of course not. Dr. Smith will be here momentarily. Don't worry. You won't feel a thing. Here's a little morphine." He held up a needle and syringe I hadn't noticed. A rubber band materialized and he tied it around my upper arm and shot me up. I told him that I needed more than most people. He gave me more. "Remove everything below your waist and I'll be right back with Dr. Smith."

I heard the door lock behind him. I stumbled upright and tried it anyway. Locked. I worried that these quacks wouldn't know what they were doing. I wondered if it was all part of Adam's plan. The Xanax and an unidentifiable pill they'd given me before bed a few hours ago—and the morphine—melted me into this feeling of fuzzy calm. Warmth shot through my body. My mother walked in through the wall and kissed my broken hair. My rubbery body fell against the table. I leaned on it to remove my green hospital pants and underwear, but left my socks on as my mother whispered I should. My ass stuck to the paper and I saw a white sheet folded on the counter. I almost fell over trying to get to it, and had to put toe-to-heel as if walking a balance beam to retrieve the sheet. I wrapped my bottom half in it, and my mother nodded that was right. I sat hiding in a corner on the concrete floor. My mother bent down over me. I could feel her damp lips touch my cheek as she kissed me before walking back through the wall.

The door opened and the two doctors entered as

if on cue. They were literally anonymous—covered in green masks, glasses, green hats, green scrubs, rubber gloves.

Dr. Smith loomed over me cowering on the floor and held out his hand, introducing himself. I didn't shake. He lifted me by the elbow and directed me to lie down on the metal table.

"Move your rear end forward," he said. I did.

Adam was touching my legs. Adam was petting my head. Our baby was about to be born. "Ready," Adam asked.

"Yes." I wondered who the baby would look like. I wondered if she was really Adam's. It sounded like someone was vacuuming. Why is Adam cleaning the house, I thought, when the baby is about to be born?

The next thing I knew I was being shaken awake for morning meds by a nurse with a clipboard. When I went into the bathroom to take a piss, I found a pad saturated with blood stuck in my underwear. Blood was pouring from my cunt. My throbbing head dropped into my lap and tears heaved from somewhere, from everywhere.

After the bleeding subsided on Wednesday I decided to try Adam again. Still nothing. Leotard woman was waiting for the phone when I hung up. She was still wearing pink. She was still wearing make-up. I still hadn't figured out why she was in but the ballet outfit seemed a good enough reason. I wondered whether I should direct her towards a stripping career. Guys dug on any sort of costume—cheerleader, nurse, French maid—aerobics instructor, why the hell not?

I especially remember this one feature stripper that came to The Veil. Star strippers came in to perform one weekend a month. Most were porn stars. They all had handmade sequin costumes that would have made Dolly Parton jealous. There were several layers to those costumes which allowed them to slowly disrobe. Hat. Gloves. Vest. Skirt. Shorts. Bra. G-string. I had one layer. Sometimes two.

Anyhow, the club paid them a few thousand to come, and they made several thousand more in tips, selling porn videos and posing for Polaroid pictures on a john's lap. They were pretty dull and I hardly noticed them at all until I saw this one poster. It read: "OLIVE! Friday and Saturday only." There was no picture, nothing. That made me think of Olive Oil. Not really a stripper. Not really a stripper's name. But then, one could never tell.

It turned out Olive was an ex-U.S. gymnast who had been training since she was six-years-old but quit after failing to qualify for the Olympic team. So she got some implants and took to the stage, where she wowed men with her flexibility. But as the years went on and more gymnasts became strippers, her flexibility wasn't such a big deal. Didn't matter. She worked up a special skill all her own.

When I got to the club that Friday night, Olive was ready to hit the stage. I stood in the crowd and waited. I wondered what this super special skill was. Then she began performing, and I thought, how boring.

Bolt Risk

Olive danced, bent and flipped for a few songs. It was no big deal. I was unimpressed. Just when I was about to give up on her the stage went dark. When the lights came back up, a giant martini glass—a round plexiglass pool on a stem, really—stood at center stage. Olive dipped a toe in it, then a leg went in and the rest of her followed, hardly making a splash. She rested naked in the glass, wiggling her feet and rubbing her tits. Her name finally made sense to me, although she looked more like a Cherry than an Olive. But then I suppose she'd be sitting in a cosmopolitan instead of a martini, and that would have been way too gay for a straight strip club.

It took a minute to see what she was up to. The first guy looked up at the ceiling, at the sprinkler system, trying to figure the origin of the stream of water that just hit him in the face. It dripped down his cheek and he wiped it off with the backside of a hand. The second guy who got struck looked downright confused. The third threw a fifty on the stage: He knew exactly what hit him—liquid shot from Olive's cunt.

So standing in the nut house looking at pink leotard lady I figured she could do an aerobic strip tease. Her body was good enough. She'd probably make bank, especially if she learned a skill like Olive's.

"Will you," she breathed, "be coming," another breath, "to exercise class?" Those seven words exhausted her. She looked like she might faint. I wondered how she could possibly exercise.

"We'll see."

She smiled and her make-up didn't crack at all.

Later that afternoon, after Ryan and I were checked off on the clipboard, we snuck into my bathroom together and did a line.

"So, what do you want to do Sunday night?" He looked at me with those bloodshot eyes and shaggy hair. He was really so cute. When I had my melt-down, Ryan pulled out a notebook of lyrics and read them to me through the isolation room door. They were good. Kind of your typical teenage angst bullshit but that was his reality. I figured his lyrics would get better the longer he was locked up. Living in hell feeds the creative process, I remembered reading in one of my mother's journals, written when she was suffering the most, from her muscle disease or from living with my father, I never knew. And here Ryan and I were, pretty close to hell. I snorted another line and realized that, no, this is OK. Rehab would really be hell.

"How about a movie? I'll spring for the popcorn," I laughed, excited about the prospect of Sunday night, when only one nurse watched the whole ward floor. "Or a dive bar. I could use a good bottle right now. I'm missing whiskey. It's starting to bum me out."

"I'm serious," he said kind of hurt, kind of young. The eight years between us suddenly seemed huge. There were a lot of ways we were different. There were a lot of ways we were the same. He snorted another line and so did I.

We bounced out of the bathroom with a minute to spare before the checker came by. It's strange to live between five minute checks. You program yourself. My head rang like an alarm clock every four-and-a-half minutes. You had to protect your limited freedom any way you could.

Ryan went to the window for a Xanax. I directed myself to the metal mesh window in the TV room which was ajar. A storm was forming. The sky was white. LA disappeared in the weather. Wind pushed under the window and I held out my hands to catch it. The red-faced girl who ripped open her arm had also been released from isolation, motivation gone. A tight white bandage was taped around one of her forearms. She stood in the doorway because she and the doorway happened to be in the same place, and nothing more.

When the crash sounded in the hallway I was jolted, she was unmoved. I skipped past her and saw attendants running, attendants yelling, nurses on the phone. When the doors opened to accept a new patient, someone had bolted.

In the middle of the hallway, beyond the doorway, the patient ran directly into an elderly doctor. The doctor went down, holding his hip, scrambling for his glasses. The police came. The white coats told the uniforms who it was: Ryan.

Two hours later Ryan returned sedated in a straightjacket. He was lucky not to know where he was. Even temporary ignorance was bliss.

Late that night, probably actually early Thursday morning, Dr. Chan woke me up again. It was time to go to the basement again. I couldn't need an abortion again, could I?

There was the table, the machine, the morphine. Everything was hazy. I felt myself being strapped into this large, looming metal throne. Thick leather belts were tightened across my head, chest and legs. Heavy metal buckles weighed against me. A man in a black hood stood behind a glass window. His hand gripped a lever. He pulled it down. My body shuddered. I smelled bacon and realized that it was the sizzle and stench of my own burning flesh. I was being electrocuted. As I nodded off into total unconsciousness, into death, I looked at the man behind the glass. He let go of the switch and pulled off the hood. It was Adam. Laughing.

I woke the next morning with a headache and limped into the bathroom. I took a piss and leaned over the sink for a drink of water, my mouth puckered dry. I lifted my pounding head and saw in the mirror that my forehead was branded by two circular bruises. My hair stuck to my skin by something that resembled dried sperm. I didn't care. I didn't care about anything.

I stood there until the nurse ordered me to go. I went. She told me to take my medications. I took my medications. She told me to go to breakfast. I went to breakfast. She told me to go to group. I went to group. Walter stabbed Sew in the cheek with a pen. Whatever. Two days passed in that sort of brainless haze.

Then it was Sunday night. This time it wasn't Dr. Chan who invaded my sleep, my dreams, but Ryan.

Bolt Risk

He was out of isolation.

"Let's go," he whispered, his breath wet in my left ear. I slid out of bed and followed him into the bathroom. He pulled the door quietly shut, and shared a few lines of cocaine. Only then did it feel like my brain was maybe functioning. Thoughts were returning. Ryan pulled down his drawers and pushed his hard dick against me. I led it inside. It felt like forever since I'd been fucked. And Ryan, he was legal, right? I figured he should at least be bar-age and here he was, with me behind bars. He thrust against me, pressing me against the sink, and began eating my face. I felt him inside of me for about two minutes—it felt impossible for me to have an orgasm anyhow—when he got soft and fell out. Teenagers were quick. Maybe the five minute checks had something to do with it. Then things got hazy, and everything started fading out.

Ryan whispered for me to follow him into the cellar. I couldn't feel my body as we crawled along the urine-yellow linoleum floor past the nurse's station. I couldn't figure out why we were crawling, because no one was around anyway. I couldn't hear the other patients' snoring in their sleep. All I could smell was piss.

We crawled down the hallway to the staircase and took it all the way down. We tiptoed into the basement hallway lit by emergency lights which turned everything red. Ryan began checking rooms at one end of the hallway, I began at the other.

There was a broom closet, a bathroom, an office with a pull-out couch pulled-out. I got a sickening

129

sensation in my stomach when I saw what had to be the abortion room. I wondered if I should open the door. I wondered if the whole thing was just a dream. This place. The pregnancy, the abortion. Adam, Hollywood. Maybe I had a miscarriage. Maybe I was never pregnant to begin with. Maybe there was no Adam. Maybe that guy down the hall is Adam.

"Hey, over here," Ryan-Adam whispered loudly. Ryan-Adam. You weren't alive in the summer of '69, I wanted to tell him. He stood in the doorway, looked in and laughed. I wandered over to see what all the fuss was about.

Inside the room hundreds of banana peels hung from the ceiling and there, sitting in the mist of the dried jungle were Fred and Walter, smoking. The smoking bananas didn't particularly smell like anything. It was just kind of eye-watering smoky.

"I was wondering when we'd see you," Fred said, and passed the banana joint. I inhaled deeply. It didn't taste like anything. A little like an ashy clove, was all. I passed it to Ryan. He inhaled.

"So, are any other rooms empty?" Ryan wanted to know.

Walter squeaked that he sometimes napped in that office with the foldout couch because he heard Dr. Chan got a lot of action in there, which was just what he was hoping for.

"I could sure use some therapy like that," he squeaked.

Fred grunted and looked contemplatively at the smoke's glowing tip. His eyes were wide and wet as he told about how he and Barbie, a former patient who had something like twenty different surgical procedures to try and look like the doll, found the basement together.

"She was addicted to shocking. When they gave her the first shock treatment, she was hooked. It made her scream like she was fucking cuming," Fred said. "We'd come down here and she'd have me stick metal plates on her scalp and crank the machine."

"The abortion room?" I asked.

"No, not abortion room. Shock room. The one that's double bolted," he said and rolled another banana.

I woke from the dream after smoking three more bananas. The tag on my shirt was stuck to my face, my clothes were inside out. I wanted another banana joint, but the check nurse said there was a message waiting for me. It read: "Call Adam. Urgent."

My head started twirling. I wondered how this could be. I called him before medication. He answered. He was in bad shape.

"Baby, I can't do this anymore. I can't do this to you. To me. I'm not sticking around. I just wanted to tell you that I love you." He was sobbing. He was insane. "I'd rather have you locked up than be with someone else. I'd rather be dead than be with anyone else."

He hung up the phone. Voice mail picked up when I tried to call back. The nurse told me to hang up the phone and get in line, I was late swallowing my pills.

I received more surprising news at the pill counter. I had been in long enough to warrant a walk. An attendant would take me and a group of five others out. It would happen once a week, as long as I behaved. We could smoke. And, best of all, Ryan was in my group.

One step outside and our insane group lit a collective smoke. Some combination of exhaust, cigarettes and tropical flowers melded to become Los Angeles. I had forgotten that smell. I was scared of it. But not as scared as I was of that Lysol stench.

Ryan and I walked together, alone, chain smoking. No one seemed to be paying much attention. I guess they figured we were too fucked up to run.

"I got this friend I can call, she'll meet us with her car," Ryan exhaled along with some smoke. "She'll say she's my girlfriend, but who the fuck cares? If we can get out of this state we'll be alright. Hey, that'd be a good chorus for a country song. I wish I had a guitar," he grinned.

"You two," the attendant shouted, probably because we were lagging so far behind. We looked up just as she turned to chase Sew. He was running circles in the middle of the street.

After the walk I sat in group therapy in a daze—a daze caused by pills, Adam, sex, maybe bananas. And then Dr. Sandwich decided to get on my case.

"So you say that you shouldn't be here. Why, then, do you think you are," she tapped her three-inch scarlet fingernails against my file.

"A breakdown in our judicial system, a loss of civil

rights, the conservative climate of the country. And then there's Adam," I slurred, and then hacked. I had a hard time seeing past her heaving breasts.

"Oh, your husband. So you blame all of this on him. You can't get better if you don't take responsibility for your actions."

I snorted, "What action? Sleeping?"

"Now, see, I can't recommend your release until you come to grips with your illness. It's been forty five days and I've seen no improvement."

"Forty five days?" I was stunned. My hands were shaking again. My brain was shaking again. I wondered whether I was still actually alive. I wondered if I was in hell. I couldn't be, though. The people in hell had to be more interesting than this.

"Maybe the problem is all these fucking drugs you have me on. Maybe the problem is that my hands won't stop shaking. Maybe the problem is that you people still don't realize that Adam is hardly a husband."

Dr. Sandwich's tits sighed. "Watch your mouth. There's no need to speak to me like that. I am here to help you, even if you don't want to be helped."

Dr. Chan was in the doorway.

"Come," he told me. "Let's go for a walk."

Our walk took us out of the ward, into the elevator, and into his private office. Dr. Chang sat down on the couch. I sat on a chair.

"Now why are you sitting so far away? Come here. We need to talk."

The moment I sat down beside him, he put his cold hand on my thigh. He rubbed it.

"Oh, you're getting too thin. You must eat if you want to get well. Your brain needs nourishment to recover."

His face was a blur as he pressed his cold fish lips against my mouth. All I could think of was sushi. He pushed me against the mattress, breathing fast. He was a pro.

"Now, if you behave, I can recommend your release. I will take special care of you at home."

Suddenly, his dick was out. It was small, stubby, useless. Fingers would be more effective than that, I thought, nauseated. He was breathing hard. He was jerking off. His hand was at work, jiggling more than stroking. Then yellow sperm spat onto on my hospital shirt. I started to involuntarily gag. He was still panting. He fell back on the couch. The whole thing was boring as hell.

"There are clean gowns in that closet. Put some on."

I opened the closet, found identical garbs and realized I had to change in front of this dick. I turned my back so all he'd see was my ass, which was probably what he wanted anyway.

Once dressed, I stood by the door, immobile.

"Did you not take your Xanax today? Perhaps you need a stronger prescription. Perhaps some morphine?"

Dick back in pants, he went over to the desk and opened the drawer. There was morphine in that drawer. I made a mental note. Dr. Chan made up the shot.

"I'll see you tonight," he said, leaving me alone

in the hallway. A nurse appeared from nowhere. It was hard to control my body, to walk back toward the elevator. I leaned against the wall of the elevator while the nurse half-watched me lean, half-watched the floor numbers flash by in neon yellow. When the door slid open he pushed me into the ward and walked away. I used the railing to direct myself to group, which was over. I sat on the stinky couch anyway.

My body relaxed into a slouch. My mind relaxed into a slouch. We were sitting there slouching on the couch when in walked a nurse.

"You have a visitor."

"What?"

"A visitor. A visitor is here for you," the nurse said in slow motion.

I stood, swayed, and staggered to the visitor's room which stood across from the nurse's station, monitored through a plate glass window. I'd never been in there before. There sat Ryan with his cocaine friends, aerobic chick and her husband. I didn't recognize my visitor until a couple of minutes after he spoke. It was Chris from the laundry room.

"What are you doing here?" Words dripped from my morphine mouth as I fell down beside him on the leather couch.

The visitor's room was the only place regular people were allowed. The furniture was new. The rose colored couches and chairs were clean. Patients were allowed in only if they had visitors. There was a two-hour window, something like four to six, that folks could stop by for a visit. They never stayed long. Not after they smelled their mother, brother, lover. Patients reeked like dogs that had the shit washed off them with Lysol for the occasion. Not at all a person from the outside world. Not at all a person. That stench was what allowed visitors to go home alone an hour later. After all, how could they think they abandoned a person who didn't smell like one?

"I ran into Zelda in the laundry room and she told me what happened. Nice boyfriend you have," Chris said.

I grinned. I thought about Adam naked. I thought about Adam playing guitar. I tried to shake Adam from my brain. I looked at Chris. He looked vaguely familiar.

"Zelda knows I'm here?"

"Everybody does. Look, I brought you something." He pulled a Snickers and a can of Diet Coke out of his bag. Sugar and caffeine. Neither of which I had had in more than a month. "And, you heard about Adam, right?"

"What?"

"He got kicked out of Z. They were all sick of his shit. Even Bob. They had to pay him off, but he's pissed. I heard Capital's looking at a solo career for him, but they're worried about his vocals, what kind of shape he's in. But *Guitar Player* did a cover story on him so maybe another band will pick him up."

"He's an asshole," I think I said aloud. Then I heard through the slur of my brain Chris say, "Drugs-women-partying-fucking-Samantha-Adam-fucking-singer."

Bolt Risk

Then he was gone. Chris was gone. All the visitors were gone. And I was directed back into the ward, back into my reality.

The next morning, I woke with teeth clenched, a pounding headache. I looked in the bathroom mirror and saw deep purple marks on my forehead.

Something had happened. I couldn't think what. I couldn't think at all.

I walked through the routine. The nurse didn't have to point me in any direction. I was a walking robot. Something was happening to my mind. It felt different, calmer. The instinct to resist pulsed through my blood, but I couldn't reach it.

Some time later I thought about Frances Farmer walking around like a zombie, defeated.

Still later I thought maybe they were frying my brain on a skillet and then returning it to my skull. I looked for evidence—scars, bald patches—but found none.

Then I remembered reading about it in college. Electroconvulsive therapy, "shock" removed from the name to dispel the perception of mind electrocution. Shock and lobotomies, the two methods of damaging the brain into submission.

Shock started when some guy realized that epileptics never had schizophrenia and figured that schizophrenia could be cured by inducing epileptic-like convulsions. Electricity is shot from one side of the brain to the other, causing patients to lose consciousness and undergo violent seizures. Bodily damage is avoided by first injecting the patient with a painkiller or relaxant, but shocks cause memory loss and brain damage. They damage your brain into submission.

At least with a lobotomy your mind was dead, your personality was dead. With shocks, memories and thoughts flashed through the brain, too fast to grasp. You saw flashes of reality distilled by white walls, white coats, white pills. You remembered re-membering reality, but didn't know what it was.

That, and the staff could fuck with you.

"I'm sure I don't know what you mean, shock therapy. We don't do that here," the check nurse ex-claimed when I asked about it.

"Then explain the bruises on my forehead," I said.

"Well, I'm sure I don't know what you mean."

Back in the bathroom with Ryan the following Sunday, mind cleared by cocaine, I asked him if he'd had any shock treatments.

"Hasn't everybody," he asked and lifted his hair. Brown bruises branded his forehead. "I kind of like it, makes me feel kind of light. The convulsions are kind of fun. That'd be a good name for a punk band, The Convulsions."

My brain suddenly started throbbing with frag-mented memories: I was belted down on the table, plates were stuck to my forehead. My mind was screaming, but my vocal chords wouldn't respond. My body was convulsing, but I couldn't move. I real-ized my brain was being slowly killed. I got scared.

"They've been frying our brains." I stated the obvious. I was becoming obvious. I was wigging out. I was completely losing it, like that time I chopped off my hair. Like the time I climbed in Adam's window. My body was sobbing. Ryan held onto me until his shoulder was drenched. Then he pushed me away. I was being a fucking pussy again. Shit.

"Tomorrow, we lag behind everyone else. I'll have Jade meet us a couple blocks from here."

I must have looked at him blankly because he said, "It's time to bolt."

5

I palmed my Xanax that morning. I wanted to be as up as possible, and anyway I'd probably want the pills for the ride. Especially if I could wash them back with some whiskey. I pulled on the clothes that I was arrested in, Adam's clothes, sat shoeless on the nasty couch and watched puffs of clouds blow by the city's polluted sky. Ryan fell down next to me. He was fidgeting. He had already called that girl Jade and was ready to go.

An attendant finally called us to the door for our walk. Our group had grown to eight. I figured that was good—the more psychos there were for the attendant to watch, the better. My body was shaking but I worked to control it, which had me moving pretty slowly anyway.

Once outside Ryan and I lit smokes and really didn't have to work at dragging ourselves behind the others. We must have looked incapable of bolting, because after the woman yelled at us a couple times we were left pretty much alone. After all, we were only zombies with smokes, not bothering anybody.

Ryan and I managed to look cool—smoking, pointing out used condoms hiding under bushes, picking up and finishing still-lit half-smokes dropped by the psychos up front—until we got to the second corner and noticed a red car idling down the street. Then we couldn't help but look each other. We were about half a block behind the rest of the group when we started sprinting simultaneously and jumped into the red BMW. The tires hollered as we took off. I thought I heard some yelling but we were heading in the opposite direction so I couldn't be sure.

Jade was pretty much bitchy to me from the moment I climbed into the car behind Ryan. She wouldn't laugh at my jokes, but pretended she was concentrating on steering. Maybe I wasn't all that funny, but Ryan thought I was. Especially when we passed the La Brea Tar Pits and I started in on how a chain-link fence was built around it because suicidal idiots were continually jumping into the bubbling tar to die. I concluded that they really didn't want to die but instead dreamed of being immortalized as fossils. Imagine that, a higher life form, many millennia from now, finding their fossils preserved in tar, Nike sneakers and all. Maybe they would conclude that the deaths by tar were accidental, just like we think it was for the dinosaurs. Maybe, really, there were suicidal dinosaurs. They saw cavemen, were disgusted, and decided to take the plunge. Or they couldn't get laid.

Bolt Risk

Ryan and I were crying we were laughing so hard as we contemplated pissing in the Silver Lake reservoir as we drove by on our way to the interstate—and I realized we really weren't too far from my apartment. But Jade refused to talk to me and scrunched up her face when I'd respond to some sentence she'd spit out. It was tiresome, but I figured since we were going to be in the car for something like seventeen hours, I'd try to be normal to her. Maybe the morphine was maintaining my mellow. Maybe it was all those shocks.

Anyhow, I liked her because she had such an attitude problem. She was this eighteen-year-old punk rock chick living off a trust fund. Jade had long black dreadlocks and a soft, round body. She wore black baggy pants and what looked like a ripped Madonna-inspired T-shirt. They were the only pieces of clothing she owned, or wore anyhow. She reeked so bad that I had to keep a cigarette lit to keep from puking. She was the perfect image of a punk rock Kewpie Doll. The whole thing was too funny.

Once we got on I-5, I inhaled a breath of carbon monoxide-flavored relief. Ryan spent his time on the Interstate sucking down cocaine and when we'd stop to get gas, Jade and I would go into the bathroom and do a few lines. She bought a couple of pints of whiskey and gave them to Ryan who shared them with me. Then I really felt better. It was all right, being with Jade, except she got blatantly bitchy when hopped up.

"I don't know why you hang out with someone as young as Ryan. Don't you have friends your own age or did you scare them all away," she said every other stop.

Funny thing was, Jade had no idea she was so right on.

Anyway, we got to Seattle pretty quickly, on account of the coke. We never stopped for more than a few minutes to fill, piss and snort. As the trip progressed Jade got even bitchier and started pushing for Ryan to dump me and drive off with her. By the time we reached Oregon he got irritated; Ryan pushed Jade aside and grabbed the wheel. He blasted Z's latest CD and gunned the engine. In between tracks he told her a zippy account of Adam's committing me to the hospital. He told her that I wasn't one to be reckoned with.

"This nurse just looked at her wrong looked at her is all and she jabbed a paperclip in his eye, stuck it right there and the guy started screaming and running around in circles like he belonged in the cage," Ryan, all coked out, lied and laughed.

At least I think he was lying.

Then he told her he was staying with me.

The story must have scared Jade because in the end Ryan convinced her to give him some cash. Or maybe he fucked her for it when they disappeared for a while in some gas station bathroom while I sat drinking in the car. One could never tell. But she looked scared when she dropped us off on First Avenue in Seattle and sped away. I saw pissed off eyes glowing in the rearview mirror as I waved a polite thank-you-goodbye.

Ryan and I decided to head up to Capital Hill

and got a room at a youth hostel on Broadway. I figured it would give us some time to find jobs, apartments. It didn't end up being a good thing for Ryan, though, because he couldn't handle being around a bunch of junkies. Within a week he ended up on the street. He didn't want to be anywhere like home, and I couldn't blame him for that.

My first full day in town I bleached out my short cut and got a waitressing job on First Hill. The owner of the restaurant was this bitchy Korean woman who charged the waitstaff for every error. The waiter even had to pay for the food if the customer didn't like it.

"You don't ring in, you pay," she said. "You write wrong food, you pay. The customer don't want it, you pay."

It sounded like a bad deal, but I was down to seven bucks. I lost some money at that job, but I made more. I was used to it from the strip joint anyway, paying to work.

The youth hostel was OK and without Ryan I saved cash by moving into a room with three other bunks. It was weird sleeping in that place with various women. I always worried that one of those chicks would slit my throat while I was asleep, but I mostly slept during the day anyway. Sometimes I got better bedding offers. The first one came from a witch.

I met him at this dive bar on First Avenue. He was this kind of warped, kind of nice regular seeming guy. He had just gotten off work. He was wearing baggy white pants, a baggy white coat and a black watch cap. His name was stitched in red thread above his breast. He said his wife was home and I could crash on their couch and watch a movie if I wanted. I figured, sure, hell, why not? We hopped a bus to the University District.

The first thing that made me think this guy might be a little strange were the black candles. They were everywhere, melting down to a deep purple. Purple and black velvet curtains embroidered with five pointed stars blanketed the windows. More candles flickered at the bottoms but didn't torch the place somehow. On the coffee table in front of the couch was a massive leather volume. I flipped through its thin pages and perused the script, but it was mostly just unreadable witch jargon.

The place was so decked out that I felt like I was on some B-movie set. The kind where producers rent a furnished Hollywood apartment in which to shoot their bad film. I had a strange experience on one of those sets.

When I got off working a day shift at The Veil a few months back, some guy who was standing outside the club said that a film was being shot down the street. Girls were being paid four hundred bucks to walk by the camera naked. It sounded like either a good deal or fucked up deal, but I figured it deserved a shot. I really needed the cash for rent so on my way home I stopped by the apartment. All of the walls were white, all of the furniture was white. It reminded me of fat Al's house, but not as nice. Anyhow, the director was another Middle Eastern guy who told me to stick around for a scene. I waited and waited. Two hours went by. Girls came and went. The scene came and went. He never called me in front of the camera. Then, after things seemed to be shutting down, I told the guy he owed me four hundred bucks.

"After dinner I will give you your money," he smirked. Fuck, man, he was looking for a prostitute. Or a girlfriend.

"No deal," I told him. "Pay up."

After endless bitching and refusing to leave until he paid up, he finally did. Dealing with that shit was hardly worth the dough. I did get my rent paid though.

But then it made me suspicious of B-movie sets— and I wondered if this guy rented out his place to filmmakers who shot low budget witch movies. I wanted to ask him but he was off talking to his wife, who was no where to be seen. A little while later he came back out with a pillow and blanket and tucked me in on the couch. Then he changed his mind, lifted my legs and sat down under me. He started talking about how he and his wife are Wiccans. He rubbed my legs and explained that they're not really witches.

"It's a religion. We believe that doing evil is against all moral laws. We do use spells though."

They sounded like witches to me but that was OK. His voice got quieter as he droned on and I drifted off into this warped vision of Hansel and Gretel.

The kids were skipping about in little ginger-bread clothing, skipping into a candy-covered iron castle. They skipped toward the fire, toward a bubbling martini glass-shaped cauldron. There they performed an erotic striptease: Gretel unrolled one stocking and then the other, Hansel bent over and slapped himself in the ass. Unclothed, they gleefully leapt into the boiling liquid like synchronized divers.

I woke with a start and saw these two cloaked figures standing there, one holding a silver chalice and the other a double-edged knife. They were chanting from the witch bible, spooky shadows under black cloaks.

Suddenly, one of the witches plunged the knife into the chalice. I half expected some sort of fiery explosion, some ghostly spirits to appear, something. But nothing happened. One of the witches simply removed the knife and sipped from the chalice. The other did the same and passed it to me. I sat up and took a sniff. It smelled like good red wine so I drank it down. Still beat I yawned, flipped over and pulled the blanket over my head. Then I went back to sleep.

The next morning I opened my eyes and saw the witches staring at me, sitting side by side in matching purple chairs. She was chubby and plain. He was balding. They wore normal people clothes.

"What's up," I yawned.

"Last night we performed the Great Rite," said the girl witch.

"OK."

"It is associated with the sacred marriage, unity with the deity. It is a magic rite of sexual intercourse," the boy witch said.

I must have looked confused because the girl witch said, "We're looking for a woman to have a relationship with. We'd like that woman to be you."

"You mean you're looking for a chick to fuck together?"

"No. A relationship," the boy witch said.

"Thanks, but I'm not sure I'm up for that. I mean, you're witches and I'm an atheist. I can't see how that would work."

They handed me cab fare back to the hostel, disappointed. I spent the whole ride thinking about my Satanic marriage to Adam, depressed. Maybe we should have heeded Stoner's warning about the moon. One could never tell.

A couple of nights later I met this punkabilly bouncer in front of some hip dive club. He was well over six feet tall and had a chipped front tooth. The wallet stuffed in the rear pocket of blue jeans was connected by a chain to his black leather belt. His hair was slicked back. He reminded me of Neal Cassady. In fact, his name was Neal. His job was fun: He mostly just hung out in front of the bar drinking beers and smoking. So I joined him. We leaned against the building for hours, drinking and smoking. Sometimes more. Sometimes he went inside and would return with a body thrown over his shoulder. He'd toss it to the curb with a 'thunk.' It was amazing. No matter how large or how small, male or female, soft or bony, everyone of those bodies made that same 'thunk' sound. By the third go around I figured it was the sound of a head smacking against the curb. After another two, I was no longer sure.

I was contemplating this when a group of five guys stopped at the door to finish up smoking a joint before heading in. Neal was still busy throwing people out of the club. The six of us were standing around, not saying much, when one of them started talking.

"What kind of music do you listen to?" he asked me. I couldn't see what he looked like, I was too drunk. He was just kind of blurry, just a blurry mouth. And I hated that question. I just wished Neal would get back with another drink.

"All genres," I slurred, annoyed.

"I mean, what's in your CD player right now?" he pressed, and I wondered, how'd he know I stole a CD player out of Jade's car?

"The Boxers," I said, and fumbled trying to light a smoke.

Then all five of those assholes burst out laughing. I mean, really started choking they were laughing so hard. It pissed me off, it reminded me of those fifth grade girls. It reminded me of my father. It really reminded me of Adam. I always felt like he was laughing at me. I thought I got away from that feeling when I got away from LA.

"Fuck you, you fucking assholes. The Boxers are the balls," I hissed.

The laughter subsided and the mouth looked like he felt bad. "No, it's just that this is Teddy Singer," he said.

I wobbled over to the boy he was pointing to, the boy who was supposed to be the band's bass player. I got right up close and looked him in the face.

Bolt Risk

"You're not Singer. Singer has got to be older than you, or dead," I said. They were silent. I felt stupid. I wanted another drink. Bad. I fell back against the building and leaned there in silence. The group filed inside, silent. It wasn't until the next day that I found out Teddy Singer was indeed in town. And sober remembered that his brother the guitarist was dead, not him. Figures.

Right after they left, Neal came out with more drinks. Relief. Then he went back in for more people. It went on like that until the place shut down. Afterwards, as we were walking to the parking lot, I asked him how long he'd been in Seattle.

"My, my, my, time does fly, 'cause ten years already gone by."

I couldn't tell if he was fucking with me, but we were at the car. It was light blue with dark blue fins. Neal opened the driver's side door and I slid across the long stretch to the passenger side of the '55 Chevy. He got in and pulled me back down next to him. He drove with his right arm stretched across the back of the seat. The top was down, the night was soggy and the mist moistened my face. As we flew down the road, I began to think that maybe this was Neal Cassady. Maybe I had gone back in time.

Then I looked down at my five-inch platinum skirt, part of an old stripper costume Chris had mailed along with some of my other shit. Nope, definitely not '50s wear. Neal just put on a good show.

He slammed on the brakes and we crashed at some chick's place. I never found out who she was, how she and Neal were connected. Maybe by the wallet-and-belt chain. All I knew was that she was in the other room fucking someone else. I heard them going at it as I passed out: A head whacking against a wall and some rhythmic hissing.

I came to just as the sun popped up, just as Neal was sitting up. He looked at me, "Last night I did somethin' and you did somethin' and now whatever I do, that somethin' will be for you, unless you don't want me to." He found a beer bottle by the side of the bed, took a pull and coughed out a cigarette butt. I laughed. He was entertaining, but I had to go.

Then there was work. The waiters at that place on First Hill reminded me of the strippers in Hollywood. Not that they were young and pretty, but they were that slutty. On my first day, each server individually snuck up to me to whisper about the others.

"She's a slut, she plays with her cats, he's a dick," said the one-eyed woman.

"She's in love with her cats, he's a virgin, she steals from the register," said the slut.

"She cut out her own eye and ate it, she used to be an elementary school teacher but lost her job because she fucked a student, he kills pets," said the cat lady.

"They're all obsessed with sex," the pet killer said.

But so what. We all made a fine espresso. And everybody smoked and everybody drank.

There were two waiters I actually liked, though. Terry left high school and ran off to Seattle after he got the shit kicked out of him for being gay in Wyoming. Jan was a middle-aged cocktail waitress from Vegas who followed a dick to town. The three of us sometimes went to bars after work to drink, smoke and trade nasty stories.

Terry was tough shit. He grew up on a cattle ranch and spent his childhood doing masculine things: herding cattle, shoveling shit, blowing horses. But after a truck full of rednecks jumped him on his way home from a bar, all that tough shit was done. Terry was in a coma for two days. He nixed plans to finish high school and when he was released from the hospital he took the next train out. He was done dealing with that ignorant shit from those ignorant people.

Jan was hot, but she was too nice. That was her problem. She came to Seattle from Las Vegas all because of this dude she met while covering a shift for this waitress who never showed. Jan was at this casino carrying a tray of drinks over to some hotshot gamblers when she fell into this twenty-something bodybuilder. You know, that steroid type with gorilla arms who's unable to stand upright. She liked that kind of guy so she just stood mesmerized as he picked up each glass on her tray drank them all down—two shots of tequila, two pints of Bass and a martini. Jan hardly cared that she lost her tips and then her job. And once Dick—no shit, that's really what his name was—ran his hand down her stockings, nothing else mattered.

After a week of fucking, Jan followed this Dick back to his Seattle home. He started beating the crap out of her within a week.

"It hasn't happened in a while," she said when we first met. But then she showed up two days later with a broken wrist. It didn't seem to bother her. Maybe she was just into that shit. Some people are.

But anyway working that restaurant allowed me to collect some cash and move into an apartment on Capital Hill. The manager pointed to a mattress leaning against the dumpster and said I could take if I wanted to. I dragged it up three floors. My room was narrow but long. A tiny refrigerator and stove were shoved together in one corner. The bathroom was down the hall, but that was OK. The small sink was a useful urinal.

My apartment was right above a lesbian dildo shop that held workshops on how to use the equipment it sold. Up the way was Value Village where I bought two plates, two bowls and two glasses, a couple of utensils and a pot and a pan for five bucks. Sheets and a blanket were another five. I got two towels for a dollar. I spent another ten on a portable television.

Suddenly, I had stuff. I had a home.

It didn't matter. I wasn't in it much. There were too many boys, too many bars. The best bar I found on Capital Hill was disguised as a sports-and-pizza joint. At least that's what I thought it was when I first wandered by. Listening to a bunch of people yell at sports on TV never appealed to me, so I continued on, but changed my mind when I saw the sign in the window: PINT SIZED RUM AND COKE $3. I turned in. The place smelled like garlic and melted cheese. Smoke hung in the air. Drunks were leaning and quite possibly had already passed out at the bar. Others cackled from behind personal pitchers of beer. There wasn't a poseur in the place. Not a one. With 15 beers on tap and dollar happy hour, there wasn't a single amateur in the place, either. A table of cross dressers with stubbly faces drank margaritas. Some had salt on the rims of their glasses, on the corners of their lips. A smelly-looking bunch of punk rock kids drinking PBR were running to and from the bathroom or playing porno videogames. Everyone left each other the fuck alone. Relief.

After the bar closed I wandered the streets of Seattle. The cat waitress warned me about the dangers of the city after dark, but I couldn't see it. I knew no one: Seattle was the safest place I'd ever been.

One of those first nights I was walking down Harvard when I saw three guys standing behind a dumpster. It was a clean, green dumpster. That dumpster looked cleaner than my Hollywood slum, clean enough to sleep in.

Two of the guys were passing a crack pipe. The third was watching and grinning. They started talking to me as I approached so I stopped to socialize. They needed to cook something up but too many cops were driving by. Well, there was always my room.

We got to my room and locked the door. This skinny black guy took a spoon out of one pocket and some tar out of the other and cooked it down to liquid with a lighter. I stopped playing attention when Kevin started talking.

He had a shaved tattooed head and was recently

released from the pen. Kevin was a junkie who stopped doing junk. He wouldn't even drink anymore—not so much because it was a parole violation, but because he figured it would lead him back to heroin. He knew these other two druggies back when he lived on the streets. He'd say "Hey," to them now and then, surprised they were still alive. With his release from jail came the realization that everyone he had known had either died or disappeared.

Then, just like that, the guys were done and all three headed out the door. I was alone. But not for long. There I was sitting on my mattress smoking pot, wondering what time the bars opened in the morning. I was thinking Eileen's opened at six for breakfast and the bar in Charlie's opened when the restaurant opened, whenever that was. There was a knock at my door.

"It's Kevin."

I opened the door. He was grinning. He looked cute. I've always had a penchant for boys with tattoos instead of hair. And then there were those guys with green hair that killed me every time, especially during those college years.

The coolest thing about my pretentious gay arts college was that it wasn't too far from CBGB's. A few hours ride, but my punk friends and I would get one of the rich kids to drive us down there, especially to see this one band called Mudfuck. I had the hugest crush on the trio—really only because the guitarist-singer had green hair, the bassist a tattooed head and the drummer green hair and a tattooed body. Actually, they weren't all that good musically. Looking at them was fun, though. They were cute.

Which is kind of how I felt about Kevin. I looked at him in my doorway, stoned, wondering who he was, where he came from.

"Have you ever been to the Space Needle," he wanted to know.

"No."

"Let's go."

We took a cab down to Seattle Center and he unlocked the door with his key. Turned out he was a security guard by day. No one was in the lobby except for a couple stoned security guards, Kevin's friends. I followed him into the elevator. The elevator stopped and I followed him up a flight of stairs. At the top of the stairs he lifted a trap door. He pulled down a ladder and climbed up. I didn't really realize I was climbing the ladder until I found myself standing on top of the Space Needle. The top of the top. The wind blew droplets of rain sideways. You could see the whole city and beyond—it glowed with fuzzy reflection in Puget Sound. The wind blew me in some direction I couldn't understand.

"Come on," Kevin urged, walking to the edge, unnerved.

"What if I blow off," I wondered. My eyes peered down and I realized the top ring formed a platform below. It would be hard to commit suicide; you wouldn't fall far enough to die on the first plunge.

I walked the perimeter and then sat with Kevin. We leaned against each other while the wet clouds touched our faces. We woke up just as the horizon appeared and laughed about the whole experience being just another kind of mile high club.

Back home, I cleaned up and went to work. Waiting tables at that restaurant on First Hill was getting old. That's about all I could say about it. The boss seemingly wanted to control me because I wouldn't kiss her ass, or at least that's what I figured. I couldn't see any other reason why she'd follow me around the restaurant, looking over my shoulder all the time. And then at closing she'd have me sit in a stiff chair in front of her desk while she added up all of my checks with a calculator and demanded money from me if it was even $1 off. Of course, I never got any money back if I overcharged. It was complete bullshit, and on this particular night she decided I owed her thirty bucks, but couldn't prove how. Every time I tried to get an explanation she'd start speaking Korean even though she knew English perfectly well. After about fifteen minutes I couldn't take it anymore so I handed her the cash. I'll pretty much pay off anyone to get them to stop harassing me, but I needed a drink after that.

Terry came up to me as I was walking out. He was folding his apron into his jacket pocket. We were headed in the same direction.

"Buck's in from Vancouver. How about going for a drink with us at The Crown," he asked. Well, I figured about the gay bar, I'll have no chance of getting laid but what the fuck. It sucks going home alone at the end of the night, but finding some asshole lying next to you in the morning is worse.

So Terry, his boyfriend Buck and I hit what amounted to this giant bar complete with a techno section, a normal bar section and a dick-sucking section. Terry said he asked Jan along but that she didn't want to come. She had a black eye, was in a good mood, and couldn't wait to get home. It was too bad, she would've had a blast. A couple thousand man-bodies packed the joint, a couple thousand bodies that knew how to have a good time. Especially in the bathroom. And I had to pee.

I tried the door that said "Women" only it was locked. I listened to the groans of some boys fucking in there for a bit and then decided it sounded like it was going to be awhile. I ran downstairs and into the men's room. It was surprisingly innocent in there.

All these boys were standing there, pants down at their ankles. The room was one big mirror, pretty much like The Veil except it was all boys. And it was free. Happiness! The boys stared straight ahead, past the urinals, at each other. There were only a couple used condoms and a small smear of shit on the floor. There was one stall. It was empty.

"Hey boys, sorry but I really've got to pee." I ran by and undid my cords to a round of cheers. A Girl! I loved those boys for those encouraging words as I pissed like a racehorse. Bathrooms are fun everywhere.

Terry was coming out of the blowjob section as I was coming out of the bathroom section. He looked happy and drunk.

"I'm going out to a car for a second," he said with glazed eyes. Terry and some preppie red-headed kid who looked just like Richie Cunningham went outside. I didn't see Terry's boyfriend anywhere. I always loved that about gay boys, how they could fuck other guys without ruining their relationship. I used to think Adam could handle that, that I could handle that. It did and didn't surprise me that we couldn't. It was just sad and depressing.

I shook Adam out of my head and tried to be happy drinking with a thousand guys who I don't want to fuck and who don't want to fuck me.

Except there appeared this one guy who was promoting Camel cigarettes with coupons for free packs of smokes, T-shirts, mugs. All he needed was a picture of your driver's license. And your phone number, he told me. He was clean and whittled down to pretty. He looked like a grown-up Calvin Klein model, but messier.

His name was Ernie and he was from somewhere, Montana. I never asked him to repeat where. It wouldn't have mattered, I didn't know anything about the geography of the place. After he took a picture of my license, he handed me all his coupons and sat down.

"They always send me to gay clubs, but so what," he told me and then ordered a drink I couldn't hear. "Guys hit on me. But everywhere I go guys hit on me. Why not get paid for it?"

Made sense to me. It was one of the reasons I became a stripper. But Ernie was getting bored with it all, he said. Super gayness had taken over his world.

Bolt Risk

"All my friends are gay. All my neighbors are gay," he said and drained a seabreeze. "Gay is becoming as boring as straight used to be. It was bound to happen."

We ditched the gay bar and went for a walk through Bobby Morris Playfield. We passed a junkie here and there, slouched on a bench, slouched under a tree. A couple of speed freaks hurried by, trying to sell anything. We sat on the wet grass, I think by third base.

It was there that I caught something out of the corner of my eye: A familiar boy-body lying on a bench. He was curled like a fetus, not moving. I got closer and saw it was Ryan. He wasn't purple but he was cold and I couldn't shake him awake. Ernie called an ambulance from his cell phone and split. Right away sirens screamed from 13th Avenue.

I sat in front of the ambulance on the way to the hospital while they worked on Ryan in back. They got him breathing, things were looking good. I told them I was his sister and only relative. I had to. I didn't want his parents involved, I didn't want the psych hospital involved. I gave Ryan my last name. I gave them my old Los Angeles address.

They released Ryan to me the next day. The doctors pre-registered him at some rehab clinic in Los Angeles. I was supposed to make sure he went directly there.

We went directly back to my room on Capital Hill. We sat on my dumpster mattress together. We both stank. We needed showers. I still had some coke Kevin's friends sold me so I pulled it out and we both did a couple lines. After that, Ryan started talking.

"Jade showed up yesterday at the park and said she was with Adam because he's playing in town and looking for you. She gave me some cash but it's gone."

Confused, I ran outside and grabbed a copy of *The Stranger* from the bin in front of my house. We flipped through it and found that yes indeedy, Adam's new band was playing Graceland that night.

We shared a shower and after a couple more lines we decided to go to the show. We wore watch caps in an effort to disguise ourselves. We rode the bus. The bus was mostly empty but we didn't feel like sitting. We stood, hanging onto hanging holders, moving with the bus. There was this giant black lady who took up two seats singing Amazing Grace. A drunk Indian sat behind her, mesmerized. They were both too stereotypical to be real, but there they were anyway. Ryan and I got off the bus, walked to Graceland, held onto our hats and paid to get in.

The band was in the middle of its set. It sounded just like Z to me. We saw Jade sitting on the edge of the stage, drinking. Ryan and I sat at a table in back with bunch of metal heads we didn't know, ordered some scotch, and started drinking. It didn't cut into the coke fast enough.

The song ended, the room hollered. Some kid up front spit beer at Adam and he spit some right back. He slurred into the microphone and started in on another song. He scanned the audience. Back and forth. Left and right, right over Jade's head. Inspecting people, inspecting faces.

164

Bolt Risk

I got paranoid. I pulled my hat down low and slunk down on the bench. I wondered whether the whole show was a set-up to get me back on that abortion table, that electro-shock table, snorting from a table, dancing on a table. Then I realized I was sitting at a table. That freaked me out. I jumped up and ran away.

The next thing I heard was the phone ringing by my ear. It startled me into consciousness. I was lying on that mattress in my own strange room. Alone. Not sure how I got there. The phone kept ringing. I got the receiver to my face. A voice told me to turn on the news. Jesus, I'm still drunk, I thought, dropping the receiver. I turned on the news. A commercial for Dial soap was just ending with a clean woman stepping from a clean shower in a clean towel with a clean smile. The screen flashed black and then the face of a different smiling woman filled it.

"Adam Bennett, the guitarist best known for his work in the Los Angeles-based hard rock band Z, sustained life threatening injures when the BMW in which he was riding crashed into Pike Place Market early this morning. He was in town last night performing with his new band, One Eyed Freaky Monkey, at Graceland. Alcohol, drugs and speed are thought to be factors in the crash, which is still under investigation. Bennett made news recently when the popular hard rock band Z dumped him because of reported excessive drug use." The anchorwoman's smile broadened. "We'll have more at noon. Bill, I hear the sun's going to break through tomorrow."

I flipped to another channel and saw a similar report. Then another. I turned off the TV and looked at the clock. Eileen's was open. It was time for a drink.

The Author

Ann Wood graduated Bennington College before
heading to Hollywood where she became an exotic
dancer. She is currently a newspaper staff reporter
at the *Provincetown Banner* and First Place Winner
of the New England Press Association Award for
Arts and Entertainment. She lives with her son,
Sam, in Provincetown, Massachusetts.

ABOUT THE TYPE

This book was set in Plantin™, named for a well-known Dutch printer of the 16th century whose font foundry turned out traditional Old Face fonts and the italic cut of Garamond. The designer Frank Hinman Pierpont (born 1860 in New Haven, died 1937 in London) created the font Plantin™ in 1913. In the style of Garamond, this font is exceptionally legible and makes a classic, elegant impression.

Composed by JTC Imagineering, Santa Maria, CA
Designed by John Taylor-Convery